Also by KR Morrison

Pride's Downfall Series:
Be Not Afraid

UNHOLY TRINITY

K. R. MORRISON

Printed in the United States of America
Cover Design: Fantasia Cover Designs
Editing: Amanda Marie
Formatting: Linkville Press

Linkville Press
linkvillepress.wix.com/home
linkvillepress@gmail.com

ISBN-13: 978-1523619207
ISBN-10: 1523619201

First and foremost, above all else, I want to thank God for the talents He has bestowed on me. I pray that I may do Him proud, and return the talents tenfold.

Secondly, I thank my Dad for raising me right. I use my unmarried name as an author to honor both him and my ancestral Clan. I thank my Mom, too, but she is in the next life and probably won't ever hold the book, but who knows...

No author gets anywhere without beta readers and encouragers. So I want to thank all of my friends and relatives who have read my offerings and have supported me.

And I want to especially thank my husband, Paul, who knew when to leave me alone while I wrote feverishly for hours on end. He's a keeper, and has been for over twenty years.

"If you stand before the power of Hell
and Death is at your side
Know that I am with you
through it all."

For God did not make Death, he takes no pleasure in destroying the living.
To exist – for this he created all things; the creatures of the world have health in them, in them is no fatal poison, and Hades has no power over the world:
for uprightness is immortal.
16 But the godless call for Death with deed and word, counting him friend, they wear themselves out for him; with him they make a pact, worthy as they are to belong to him (Wisdom 1: 13-16)

PART 1 - CAIN

Outside of the Garden

CHAPTER 1

Cain sat in the dust and watched his parents work. The sun blazed down on them as they gleaned what little food they could find in the first drought of their exile. What used to be as easy as breathing now took back-breaking labor and long hours. He scowled as he watched them, and swatted at the ever-present flies that buzzed around his head. *It just isn't fair. So my parents made a mistake and plucked the wrong fruit off the wrong tree. What was the harm, and why am I exiled when I haven't done anything wrong? Surely I should be able to spend time in that wonderful garden my parents keep talking about instead of being out here.*

Oh, he'd heard the story many times. Father and Mother never tired of telling him and his brother of how life used to be. Every time he heard it, instead of wanting to make sure he remained obedient (which was the reason behind the oft-repeated tale), he yearned to find "paradise" and return to the ease and comfort of that former life. After all, he was nearly a man himself now, almost as tall as his father. Why shouldn't he have his chance at living in its bounty? Surely, he told himself, he wouldn't make the same mistakes his parents did. Not after the experiences they had had out here.

A noise distracted him from his daydreaming, and he frowned as his brother came into view.Abel. The very name sickened him. Such a golden boy, always willing to do whatever he was told. Never thinking beyond what this small area of their existence might hold. *Now what is the little family pet up to?*

Abel ran to his parents, and Cain could see he had been lugging something rather heavy. Having stayed in the relative coolness of one of the few trees in the vicinity, he couldn't quite make out what Abel was proffering to them. His curiosity got the better of him, and he stepped out of the shade to amble nonchalantly towards the trio.

As he approached, Cain could see what his younger brother had been laboriously carrying. It was a large rock, with a deep basin carved by nature into the top. Abel had filled it with water from a spring near their dwelling, and had toted it all this way in the hot sun. Mother and Father, grateful to Abel for his generous deed, took turns drinking thirstily from the basin as Abel held the heavy stone.

Cain felt a little parched himself. He stepped up and addressed his brother. "Abel, did you bring enough for me? After all, I'm out in this heat also."

The disdain in Cain's voice did not affect Abel at all. He was all innocence as he asked Cain, "Oh, have you been working to bring in food along with Mother and Father? I'm sorry I didn't know, for I only brought enough water for them."

Cain sneered at Abel, not caring what his parents thought of his reaction. "Of course I haven't been pulling at plants and chopping at roots. It's too hot to do such things. Food-gathering should be done when it's cooler, so it is more comfortable to work."

Adam touched Cain's shoulder. "We must work when we can, for we do not know what kind of heat or cool, dry or wet, will come tomorrow. We must..."

"I know!" shouted Cain, slapping his father's hand away. "'We must work by the sweat of our brow for our own survival,'" he mimicked. "I've heard it over and over. You want food? Fine! I'll help get some. But I'm not going to pick at trees and bushes, scrabbling in the dust." With that outburst, Cain stomped away from his astonished family.

He'd only gone a few steps when he suddenly stopped, whirled around, and marched back, his face black with fury. He grabbed the water-stone from Abel's hands. With all his might, he lifted it above his head and screamed fury at his brother. "I'll show you how to use this rock properly!"

Abel flinched and ducked, covering his head with his arms. It looked to everyone as if Cain was going to strike him with it. Adam and Eve rushed to stop Cain with cries of alarm.

Cain merely lowered the rock, and, with a malicious gleam in his eye, turned on his heel and walked away. Soon he was no more than a shimmering blot in the waves of heat emanating from the dry ground.

Those left behind watched him go. Eve spoke first.

"Why does he behave this way?" she wondered. She put an arm across Abel's shoulders, and noticed that he was trembling. Turning his chin with her hand to look at his face, she realized that he was crying.

"Oh, Abel," she whispered comfortingly, holding him close, "no, don't cry. Why are you crying?" She looked more closely at him. "Are you hurt?"

"No, Mother," Abel hiccupped, rubbing at his eyes as he tried to gain control of himself. "I'm crying because my brother is angry, and I don't know the source of his anger. Was it something I did? Was it because I didn't bring him water?"

"Son, please, you did nothing wrong." Adam joined his mate in consoling their son. "Cain did nothing to earn the water, so he should not have demanded anything of you."

The three of them watched as Cain's silhouette disappeared into the barren hills.

Another pair of eyes watched the rebellious youth as well. As Cain walked by, muttering to himself and kicking at the dust, the creature behind those eyes smiled to itself, flicked out its forked tongue, and returned to the shade of a hollow under a boulder.

It waited.

As his anger cooled, Cain began to realize how far he had stomped away from his home and family. The shadows were lengthening as the sun drew closer to the horizon. He knew he had to get back or risk being attacked by hungry night animals. Cain had heard them while lying awake at night, glad of the protection of the light created by the fire they kept blazing. He'd hear ferocious roars, followed by the pitiful scream of some unwary, weaker beast.

The youth's anger rose again, remembering how the animals had supposedly been before the exile. His parents said that all creatures had gotten along well together, grazing on the green grass of the sheltering hills instead of killing each other for survival. Now he was in constant fear of these same animals—again, not his fault. Yet it all fell on him; he could not trust the night or the animals that moved about in it.

Cain jumped at a rustling sound in a clump of tall, wind-seared grass. Fearing the possible assault of some huge beast, he tried to run. Unfortunately, he was still carrying the rock he'd taken from Abel, so he wasn't making much speed away from the threat.

This stupid rock! Why was he still carrying it? What good had taking it done, besides giving him the satisfaction of seeing his brother cower before him? Cain was about to cast it aside, when the grasses parted and out stepped a small goat.

The youngster had seen goats before, but never at such close range. With those horns on its head, he wasn't sure if this was a dangerous animal or not. He looked at the rock he still clutched in his hands. It was about the same size as the goat's head. An odd idea was taking shape in Cain's mind.

He had thrown rocks this size at trees, and had seen the marks they'd left in the trunks and branches. Would a rock stop this beast before him, if it attacked?

Another movement through the grasses, and a smaller goat emerged, nuzzling up against the first one. Cain watched as it put its head under the larger one's body and pulled at an outgrowth of flesh. Milk soon covered the outside of its little mouth.

Cain was momentarily distracted as he watched the two animals together. The larger one remained motionless as the baby drank its fill of the milk provided by its mother. *If animals could feed from the milk of each other*, Cain wondered, *why did they feel that they had to kill and eat each other also? Couldn't they just be content with the use, rather than the death, of other animals?* They all used to just eat the grasses of the fields, according to the tales of his parents.

So, the thought continued, *why did some animals eat others?*

Then it struck him, and it made sense the moment the thought occurred to him. Weren't the flesh-eaters bigger and more powerful than those they ate? If so, Cain thought, then he should eat other animals too, so that he could become more powerful than the mysterious night animals that he so feared.

He approached the creatures, which remained motionless; they had never seen a human and had no reason to distrust one. All too late, a reason was born—as the rock Cain had lifted high above his head came down upon the head of the smaller animal with a heavy thud.

The goat fell without a sound. The mother, with a frightened bleat, ran headlong into the grass.

Cain tentatively approached the little body, not knowing if the creature would get up or remain still. It was truly dead, its head split open by the weight of the rock. Not knowing what to do from here, Cain sat at a short distance and regarded the still figure.

How did one eat this animal once it was dead?

The flapping of a large pair of wings shook Cain from his reverie. A large black bird with a featherless red head landed next to the goat and, heedless of the human sitting agape nearby, stuck its beak into the carcass's head.

Cain rushed at the bird, yelling and waving his arms. It regarded him with a baleful eye for a brief moment, then resumed feeding. Picking up another rock, Cain eyed the large predator, which carried on, ignoring the extra attention. Aiming carefully, the boy flung the rock towards the bird.

It glanced off the vulture's back. The great scavenger flinched, hopped away awkwardly a couple of steps, and then returned to the goat. With its sharp beak, it tore a hole in the carcass's belly and started feasting on the exposed organs.

Cain had never seen the insides of an animal before. His family ate only what they could pluck from trees, vines, and bushes, or whatever they could dig from the ground. He moved closer, curiosity overcoming the revulsion he felt at the stench of blood and the sight of the torn body.

A few feet away, hidden from sight, the snake watched. It knew. Cain was the one. It slithered to within touching distance of the boy, and sent up its whispered voice like venom to Cain's subconscious.

"This is your kill. Why are you leaving it to this lesser species? Take what is yours."

Cain listened, the sight before him making him oblivious to the reptile beside him. He acted without a second thought. The bird lay dead in an instant. Cain had sprung forward and strangled the predator. *Now I am the hunter*, he thought, *and all others are now the hunted.*

Perceiving other large birds hovering above him, Cain knew he had to move the goat carcass to a safer spot, away from their ceaselessly searching eyes. He dragged the kill to the shelter of a nearby boulder, and contemplated how best to make use of the animal.

A noise disturbed him, and he looked out to where it was coming from. The sight almost sickened him. Four vultures had descended to the dead bird, and were in the process of eating the carcass as fast as they could. Other, smaller animals paced nearby, out of the birds' reach but waiting their turn. Cain could see them grimacing warnings at each other, their razor-sharp teeth glinting in the twilight glow.

The voice wove its way into his mind again. *"Eat or be eaten. Destroy or be destroyed. Look beyond."*

Cain looked.

The smaller animals suddenly scented danger and ran off. In the cooling breeze of the approaching night, larger shapes came closer. As they slunk nearer, their details became clear: four-footed, with bristly hair and long, sharp fangs. They circled the vultures, which were so intent on their feeding that they knew nothing of these new threats. The four-footed animals suddenly rushed on them. The birds squawked their anger, but flapped away as the creatures closed in.

All but one, which fell victim to the swipe of a large, clawed foot.

It was clear to Cain. Many predators were out there, and to stay alive he and his family had to dominate them. To kill or control them was the only way to do this. He had to go home and make this clear to the others.

Slinging the goat carcass across his shoulders, Cain slipped out from under the shelter of the boulder and, keeping an eye on the creatures at their feast, he hastened away from the sight. The sounds of the animals fighting and snapping over their scavenged meal soon grew fainter, and then disappeared.

Led on by a voice whispering in the night air, Cain followed without question. He was too busy thinking about the events of the day. How easy it was to take care of one's own needs. He should have struck out on his own earlier. However, his family needed to learn to take control of their world. He owed them that much. Then he would leave and maybe find others like himself. He refused to believe that they were the only humans in what he could perceive was an enormous land.

It took another rotation of the sun, but Cain finally made it back to his family's hearth. Considering all of the detours and dead ends he stumbled into on the way back, he was grateful that he had found it again.

He saw his parents, hacking down the brown grasses and gathering them into stacks. Abel was hauling the bundles to the dwelling place. Cain sneered in his brother's direction. Always taking orders, never thinking for himself. Well, he'd show their parents who was the most enterprising.

He called out to them while he was still a ways off, and his father ran to him, arms outstretched. "Cain! Where have you been? We are so glad you are home..."

Adam stopped short with a look of fear and uncertainty on his face. He peered at the mass of fur and blood over Cain's shoulders.

"What...what is that?" He pointed at the goat.

Cain smiled triumphantly. "This, Father, is what will ensure the survival of our family." He threw the carcass at the feet of his father. As Abel and Eve came up behind Adam, Cain bestowed a triumphant grin on all of them.

"This," he continued, "is how we will stay alive. I have learned something important in the last couple of days. I now know that killing and eating the animals that are plentiful around us will make us stronger than them. They will also learn to fear us, and we won't have to be afraid of them anymore."

Adam looked from the goat to his son, puzzled. "How could this be? We are given the growth of the trees and the plants. That is enough."

The grin disappeared from Cain's face, to be quickly replaced by the old exasperation and sullenness he usually displayed. He rolled his eyes. "Don't you understand? I've seen how these animals act. One kills, another takes away by killing, and yet another takes that from the next. If we are to survive, we must do the same."

Eve touched one of the goat's hooves. She recoiled at the stiffness of the death that enveloped it. "And why would we want to eat it?"

Idiots all, Cain thought to himself. *Why do I try?*

He made another effort to make them understand. "Obviously, eating weaker animals makes the attacking ones stronger. We want to be the strongest, so to do the same thing would give us dominance over all other animals." Cain was running out of patience.

Suddenly, to his surprise, Abel tentatively approached the fly-infested heap on the ground before them. He squatted down and looked more closely at the dead animal. Cain's hopes rose. Would his brother help sway the argument for once? "Why does it seem so alive if it's dead?" Abel poked at the exposed organs. The surface squirmed and writhed as if the viscera had indeed come back to life on its own.

Puzzled, Cain looked more closely at his prize. What he saw filled him with a mixture of horror and curiosity. Maggots filled the cavity of the now-putrefying carcass. Hiding his revulsion, Cain simply put his hand in among them, and pulled out a handful. Not knowing what to expect, yet not wanting to seem weak to his family, he opened his mouth and filled it with the writhing worms. He bit down on them.

Not that bad, really.

Smiling to show that he was enjoying his snack, he pulled on one of the goat's legs to find more maggots. The leg came off in his hand, for the meat was rotting quickly in the heat of the day. *"Eat it. Show them."* came the whisper in his head, urgent in its demand. Cain bit into the limb, and, to the horror of those standing there, chewed the meat and swallowed it.

Again, not too bad. Different, but not terrible. "Try it." He offered some to his father.

Adam took it apprehensively. While everyone else looked on, he took a bite. The taste did not agree with him. He spit it out onto the desert floor. Adam looked apologetically at his son. "I'm sorry. I just couldn't swallow the being of another living thing."

Cain seethed. If his father rejected it, the others would not try it either. He stared down dully at the carcass as his family walked away.

He kicked at the dead creature, thinking to himself.

What if there was another way to dominate these animals? How could they be of use, and still know that he was in control of them? Since his idea of killing and eating them hadn't won over his family, could there possibly be another use for these creatures? He didn't relish the idea of going back to hacking at roots, now that he had had his experience in the desert.

It came to him: an idea that would salvage his enterprise while being of use to his family.

What if he could pull the milk from the goats instead of just killing and eating them? He thought back to the memory of seeing the baby drinking from its mother.

His family was always thirsty, and it seemed there never was enough water nearby. Someone always had to run a distance to fetch seemingly tiny quantities of water. And someone, usually himself, was left out when it came to dispensing the valuable fluid.

What if they had these beasts nearby to pull milk from? Better yet, his family would be beholden to him to get the milk for them, since they wouldn't know how to approach the animals. Perhaps he would finally get the respect and admiration he felt he so richly deserved. He would rise above that brother of his in the eyes of their parents. His eyes glittered and his smile returned as he thought of how he would go about putting his plan into action.

He set out again early the next day, intent on finding more goats. He wanted to accomplish his mission while the sun was still low on the horizon. Otherwise he would be battling the white-hot heat of the day and the relentless dust and flies that made life miserable for him.

It didn't take long to find a herd of the creatures foraging in the scrub of a sheltered hillock. Cain sat back on his haunches and studied them. Perfect. Just the right amount for his purposes. Not too large a herd to handle, but not so small that, if attacked, the entire group would perish. How to get them to where he wanted them to go was another matter.And how had he instinctively known how many was enough? He tried not to think about that, for it would take him places in his mind that he would rather ignore. Someplace and Someone he didn't want to ponder.

Working from what he'd learned previously, Cain shouted and ran at the herd, flailing his arms. They scattered everywhere, most of them running around to the other side of the hillock. Cain hissed in frustration. He followed the larger group to where they had settled, inside a three-sided enclosure created by the erosion of the higher ground around it.

How to get them to go where he wanted them to? He sat on a rock and wrestled with the question.

The snake, never far away, was about to insinuate another thought into Cain's head, when a flash of light caused it to hiss and retract into the shadows. The light formed itself into the figure of a small boy dressed in white, with golden hair and luminous eyes. He radiated the light as he stood by Cain, who did not notice him there. The boy whispered into Cain's ear, and a look of comprehension replaced the worry on the would-be goatherd's face.

Cain jumped up, joyous. Laughing, he circled around to the back of the herd. Clapping his hands, he was rewarded by the sight of the goats herding together and heading in the direction he wanted them to go.

As the young man, now the self-styled family goatherd, and his flock headed towards the family hearth, the young lad watched him go. He turned to the shadows where the snake hid. The boy's eyes held the wisdom of eternities as he addressed the snake.

"He is still Mine."

The reptile twisted in the dust, fear and hatred in its basilisk eyes.

"Not for long," it hissed. "He certainly didn't praise You for Your help. I doubt he ever will. He is not like his father, groveling before You in helplessness."

Unblinking, the Child replied, "You will not win. No matter how many years and centuries go by, no matter how many souls you think you have taken from Me, you will ultimately lose,unless you come back to Me and forsake your pride."

With no answer, the snake slithered away. It glanced nervously behind itself at the Child, who slowly faded from sight, His eyes boring into the reptile.

CHAPTER 2

Abel was the first to see them. Since the shimmering horizon only delivered up dozens of black shapes, the sight filled him with fear. He ran to his parents, the fright so visible on his face that Eve dropped the harvest she was carrying and ran to him.

"Abel! What is it?" She grabbed his shoulders as he tried to gasp out what he had seen.

"Animals!" he finally choked out. "Many, coming at us. I could not tell what kind. Why would they come like that?"

Adam had also dropped his bundle and had rushed over to where Eve held her son. She turned frightened eyes to him.

"Adam?" There was fear in her voice now too. Predators had always kept their distance from the small family. Why would their behavior change now?

Swallowing his own fear, Adam said, "Perhaps they are just looking for food and water. Let them come, and we will see what they do." Yet he picked up a large stone, just to be ready.

Abel did likewise. Eve chose a stout branch from under a nearby tree. The three of them watched, trembling, as the forms took shape. Fear turned to surprise when the tallest of the mass turned out to be Cain. He was making these animals...goats!...head towards them. Was he crazy? What was he trying to do?

Adam walked towards Cain, confused and apprehensive. He glanced at the goats, especially eyeing their sharp horns, and walked a considerable distance around them to his older son.

"Cain! What is this? Why...how...these animals...?"

Cain favored his father with a triumphant grin.

"I wanted to show you, Father, that these animals can be important to us, and..."

"Cain, I told you, we will not eat these creatures."

"And you don't have to. Look."

Cain pointed to a mother goat and her kid. The baby was nursing hungrily, milk running down its little face.

"We are always looking for water, while these creatures carry drink within them. If we keep these animals around, we will never be thirsty."

Eve, who had come up behind Adam when it looked as if the goats were not going to attack, regarded the baby as it fed from its mother. She put out a hand tentatively, and the mother nuzzled it. Eve smiled.

She looked at Adam. "I think Cain is right. We can have these goats follow us and we can take some of their drink when we need it. Not having to always look for water would be one less thing to worry about. She turned to her son. "Cain," she asked him, "how did you get these beasts to do what you wanted?"

Cain smiled proudly. "I just watched them for a few minutes, and it came to me to get behind them and make some small noise. They just started walking in the direction I wanted them to go."

Abel went up to one of the goats at the edge of the herd with some grass in his hand. He nervously offered it to the goat, which bleated and took it from his fingers.

The young man stood up and raised his eyes to Heaven. "The Creator has given you a wonderful gift. We must thank Him."

Cain scowled at his brother. "Do you think I couldn't figure this out by myself?" he shouted at Abel. He had no patience for this sort of disregard for his newly-found talent.

Adam laid a hand on Cain's shoulder. "The Creator gave you the intellect and the courage to do this for the help it gives to our family. Don't you see that?"

Cain pushed his father's hand away, glaring at him. "I didn't see or hear anyone else when I decided to do this. I figured it out on my own. Why do you continue to praise and thank Someone who threw us out of a plentiful garden into this wasteland? I tell you again, *we are on our own!!!* Why can't you see that?"

Adam and Eve knew better than to continue with this argument. Nothing they had ever said or done could get Cain to change his mind. Abel, however, filled with a child's love of his family and his God, would not let the issue lie. He followed Cain and his flock to the shelter of a small group of stunted trees, arguing his point as only the innocent can.

As Cain and Abel grew, so did their abilities and their prowess with their chosen professions.

A few years into his manhood, Abel became conscious of the fact that plants and grasses grew at various times of the year, and they all held the means for their own regeneration within themselves. The challenge was to get the food-bearing plants to grow when and where he wanted them, and to protect the young shoots from foraging animals when they did begin to grow.

Animals such as Cain's goats. They had become numerous, and as such were voracious pests. The two brothers quarreled over this one issue on a regular basis. Until one day, after a particularly heated argument, Cain stalked off, away from everyone. He'd had enough. How was he supposed to keep his family happy and his goats from eating everything in sight? Had it even been worth it, starting this herding in the first place, if all that ever happened was that he got yelled at for their behavior?

For a reason he couldn't fathom, his thoughts went back to when he had first seen the herd, all backed up against the bottom of a cliff face they couldn't climb. It had made the gathering of the flock very easy.

So what if...he considered where this line of reasoning was going...what if Abel were to put big rocks up around his plants? The goats, and other land animals, wouldn't be able to reach them.

He ran back to Abel, who was currently shooing yet another goat out of his garden area. He looked up darkly at Cain. "Another one. I've asked you to keep these animals away. This food is our livelihood!"

Instead of countering with an angry outburst, Cain reached down and picked up the little goat. He smiled at his brother. "I have an idea, Abel. I have seen that my goats, and other walking animals, do not like to climb over rocks. If you put rocks around your garden, as high as their heads, your plants would be safe."

Abel thought about this for a moment and then, grinning, he clapped his hands happily.

"Yes! That would work. Come help me and we can get most of it done before nightfall."With a look of utter contempt, Cain merely turned and walked away, carrying the struggling goat. "Sorry, brother, but I must tend my goats. They need to be moved to another area so they don't bother your garden." Cain smiled smugly to himself.

As did the serpent, constantly watching.Abel watched dejectedly as his brother strode off. Oh well, it was *his* garden. Not Cain's. Cain wasn't responsible.

A vague hissing in the wind, and then a faint voice in Abel's head. It whispered, "Your brother is certainly lazy. He put the whole burden of collecting rocks and forming barriers around your garden squarely on you. It's his fault it needs to be done in the first place. Go and pull him back over here to help you. Tell your parents how cruel he is to you."

Abel shook his head, hard. "No! I will not have these thoughts. They are against the laws of love. I love my brother and will not say anything bad against him."

The snake recoiled. It knew Abel was a challenge, but sometimes the fervor with which the young man fought back was so strong as to cause the serpent pain—and it was not accustomed to pain. It looked out again from its hiding place, and hissed in surprise.

The garden wall was already half-built! Abel was accompanied by several beings, in the forms of young men, who seemed to produce boulders out of the very air. They placed the rocks in such a way as to prevent any holes in the barrier they erected. When they were finished, seemingly seconds later, Abel knelt low on the ground in gratitude. The young men placed their hands on him in a blessing, and then disappeared in a column of white light.

The next day, Cain, Adam, and Eve were awakened early by Abel. "Come see! Quick! The Creator has given us a gift!"

His parents got up without delay at those words, while Cain merely rolled his eyes and grumbled. "There he goes with that 'gift' thing again. Well, I'm not getting involved."

However, the cries of surprise and gladness from his parents spurred him to full wakefulness, and he stumbled over his feet as he ran to catch up. He'd always been jealous of his younger brother's favor with their parents; he was not going to allow Abel to make even more points with them. Not if he could help it.

When Cain got to where his family stood, he was astounded at what he saw. Not at the wall, which they'd seen and exclaimed over the night before. The surprise was what was inside.

Abel's garden, exposed to the harsh elements and stunted by the constant invasion of the goats the night before, was now miraculously transformed. Every plant was lush, its fruit or grain abundant and ready for the harvesting. It was as if Adam and Eve's previous homeland had been returned to them.

The four of them wandered among the plants, astounded at what they saw. Right there, among the ripeness of the yield, they plucked and ate their fill. Sunlight filled their patch of garden, and they basked in its gentle morning light.

Abel spoke first. "I am so grateful to the Creator. What can I do to show my gratitude?"

Adam answered, "Take these first-fruits and offer them to Him away from the garden. This will prove to Him that you trust that He will provide more."

Cain suppressed a snort of derision.

Eve looked at her oldest. "Son, perhaps you should do the same. After all, your herd is getting bigger. We never go thirsty, and when the animals die, we use their fur and bones for our own use. This too is a gift."

That, and they're rather tasty, thought Cain to himself. He always ate the remains of goats that died or were killed by predators. Not that his family knew this...

"Son?"

He shook himself from his reverie. "Oh. Yes. Of course." He wandered away. It was no use arguing with them; he'd learned that years ago. The trick was to merely ignore them when they got all spiritual like this.

"Well, there are enough goats," he mused to himself. "I suppose I could spare an old one that's about to die anyway."

He came up to the herd, and was surprised to see another human. Never had this occurred before. As far as Cain knew, his family was alone in this land. The man was standing peacefully watching the goats, a gentle smile playing over his features.

"Who are you? What do you want?" asked Cain, instinctively on the defensive.

The man looked at him, unperturbed. "The Master has sent me. He would like you to offer that goat," he pointed at one of the healthiest and strongest rams in the herd, "for your sacrifice."

Cain crossed his arms and stared at the stranger. He felt no sense of awe at the presence of a heavenly being visiting them. His heart was hardened to anything outside his own reality. The serpent had done its job well.

Well, that makes sense, Cain said to himself. *I guess if the "Creator" wants to send messengers, He can do it. That doesn't mean I have to pay attention to the message. Send this back to your Master, stranger:* "No."

The man's eyes widened, and Cain thought he heard a hiss of laughter just behind himself.

"You must. The Master wishes your allegiance. You are very close to losing your life with Him."

Cain exploded with all of the pent-up rage and resentment he'd kept inside ever since he could remember. He had raged before, but this was a reaction that went completely beyond his control. Even in his anger, he was astounded at what came out of him.

"My allegiance? Why should I ally myself with a *Master*," he sneered the word, "who makes my life such a daily burden? Leave my goats and me alone. "I am the master of me. Myself! I will decide what kind of symbolic 'sacrifice' I will make, and that is only to keep my family from bothering me."

He strode into the flock and grabbed an old she-goat by the horns. The animal, half-blind and lame, did not offer any resistance. Cain dragged if off to where Abel was setting up his altar.

A low chuckle emanated from beneath a stone outcropping. The serpent darted out its tongue from the shade.

"Now what do you plan on doing? Your Master has lost. Cain is mine."

The young man looked sadly at Cain's retreating back. The goat started fighting the hold on her, as if she knew her demise was coming.

"No one in the Master's kingdom can force Cain to love Him. Bending man's will forcefully comes from you." He turned to the snake. A fire blazed in the heavenly being's eyes. "Cain is not lost yet. No one is, until God judges the departed soul. Keep that in mind, worm. As long as he lives, as long as his soul remains bound to this world, Cain has a chance for redemption."

The snake slithered off, following Cain. An idea was forming in its mind, along with a feeling of fullness in the area above its fangs. An acrid taste wisped through its mouth. It smiled.

Cain watched as his brother selected only the fullest, least-blemished produce in his garden. The harvest was laid on a flat stone in a cleared area. His efforts complete, Abel then knelt before the pile he'd made. Bowing low, Abel praised his God loudly and gladly. Cain turned away.

The smell of smoke drifted into his nostrils, and Cain jerked back around to stare at the scene before him. The vegetation had caught fire on its own, and was being consumed by the heat. The smoke was caught up to the skies in a white column. The two brothers watched as the sacrifice was accepted by the heavens above.

The goat under Cain's hand cried out, bringing him back to the task at hand. He picked up a rock, sending it smashing down between the animal's eyes. It died instantly. He laid it out on the ground and knelt in the same fashion as Abel had. Making some half-hearted attempts at prayers, for show, he looked upon the goat and waited.

Nothing. Not even a trickle of smoke or wisp of flame.

He looked over at Abel, still prostrate on the ground. The fire had consumed the entire sacrifice. Disgusted, Cain stood up. *Well, there it is*, he thought. Even God didn't want him.

He stepped back, meaning to pick up the goat carcass and carry it behind a low hill, where he would eat as much of it as he could.

Unfortunately for Cain, he stepped directly on the snake, which was waiting for this moment.

It shot its fangs out and embedded them in Cain's heel. The venom shot forth before the shouting man could shake the creature off his foot. As Cain fell to the ground, the snake slipped away, a permanent grin fixed on its reptilian face.A feverish madness came over Cain immediately. Dark thoughts invaded his mind. He writhed, screaming, on the ground.

Abel ran to his side. "Cain! What happened? Brother, what is wrong?"

Cain stared up at his brother. The darkness overwhelmed him, and before he could stop himself, he had Abel's throat between his strong hands, and he was squeezing. Abel's face turned red as he gasped for breath.

Now it was Cain who was above his brother. Abel lay lifeless on the ground, his hair fluttering in the wind. Cain panicked. He slapped Abel, trying to wake him. Looking over at the homestead, he could see his parents running in their direction.   He saw no other way. His brother lay at his feet, lifeless. In his panic, all reason left him. Limping on his swollen foot, he turned and ran as quickly as he could, into a desert that swiftly folded him in its hot embrace.

CHAPTER 3

Cain stumbled blindly on in the heat of midday, the combination of the relentless sun and the snake's venom coursing through his body fogging his thoughts in a poisonous, mind-altering miasma. He didn't know what was real and what were dream-shapes.

He fell over a tuft of tall grass, which in his mind came alive and tried to attack him. He scrabbled across the desert floor, screaming, covering his head with his arms as he saw what he imagined to be a horrible, shapeless monster bearing down on him. His legs kicked at the beast, which cried out as it grabbed Cain's arms.

"Cain! Son!"

Cain blinked as the monster re-formed into his father. Adam was shaking him, but not in anger. Concern filled his eyes. The look changed to relief as his son regained his senses.

"Cain! What happened? Why did you run?" Tears filled Adam's eyes. "Your brother is dead!"

A dark impulse, aided and abetted by the poison in his body, made its way into Cain's subconscious. It surfaced quickly and took over any reason he had left. Adam fell back in surprise as Cain pushed him away. As he landed on the ground, he stared in horror as Cain picked up a large rock. He gestured with it wildly as the darkness exploded from him. "Leave me! How do I know what happened? Am I his keeper? I tend goats, not my over-pious brother! So he's dead. Well, he's probably happy about that. More of a chance to show you just how rotten I am in comparison. "Now go. Leave me! I don't need you, or your God. He left us long ago; I have no allegiance to Him."

Cain threw the rock at his father. Adam held up his arms in defense, knowing the strength in his son's arms. If that rock hit its target, Adam knew he would soon be joining his younger son.

The rock whistled through the air, straight at Adam's head. Cain smiled as he watched for the inevitable contact of stone with flesh. He had gotten to be an expert at such art; hours in the field entertaining himself hitting targets such as trees, boulders, and the occasional goat had honed his aim to a deadly accuracy. So he was mightily surprised when the missile, instead of braining his father, went right through him. Mouth agape, Cain stared as his father dissolved into desert heat.

Just as quickly, another form took his place. A mere child, small and fragile as the new shoots of grass in the springtime, stood staring at him. Cain, for his part, saw this new presence as just another thing to destroy. Something had changed in his mind; something evil and dangerous had overridden any of the humanity that had made him who he was. If it existed at all anymore, it was a tiny voice unheeded in the countless, swirling thoughts and commands now possessing him.

With his will overcome, and gladly, Cain gave in to the darkness. *It seems to suit me somehow*, he thought. He smiled with evil intent, and grabbed the child by the throat. Knowing nothing but a need to destroy life, Cain throttled the boy as he had Abel.

Instead of fighting him, which is what Cain wanted, the boy merely locked eyes with him. Cain, all strength suddenly gone, fell into the gaze of the child. He was instantly overwhelmed, overtaken, and surrounded inside and out by a sensation of peace, warmth, and love. He floated in a sea of beauty and calm; all hatred, pain, fear, and frustration gone.

Next to him floated the child he'd tried to kill. Suddenly, Cain realized that this being was not of the earth. The boy floated away from him, and flew to the side of another. Cain was utterly astounded to see that it was his brother, drifting along in this sea as well. However, Abel didn't see Cain; his enrapt gaze was only for a light that beckoned to him. A light that blazed brighter than the sun, but did not burn.

Abel was pulled into the light—and then he was the light. He hadn't disappeared, he had simply become one with it. Cain reached his arm toward where his brother had gone, hoping to follow him. Instead, he suddenly found himself once again in the harsh reality of the desert. He was prostrate before the feet of the child.

"Cain," said the child, in a voice terrible and powerful. It echoed through time and space, at once new and ancient, childlike and eternal. "Where is your brother?"

Cain knew better than to answer. In his blackened, evil-tainted heart, he knew that the being before him had read his mind and tried his soul. Cain cowered, his face covered, and said nothing. He dared not look up into those terrible eyes. For he knew, at last, Who addressed him. His actions were known, his life laid bare, and his secrets exposed to the light of day. Now, at what he thought was the last, understanding poured into him.

The being spoke again, and Cain trembled, awaiting judgment and vengeance.

"You have killed your brother, heedless that the power to give or take life is Mine alone."

Despair shook the man on the ground. He was sure that he was about to be obliterated from existence, along with the memory of his ever having lived at all. "Leave this place."

What? Cain couldn't believe his ears. He was being given a second chance? Was it possible?

"Live in solitude, learn from your wretched, abominable actions. Turn to Me and live. Despise the evil that surrounds you, and I will take you to Myself again."

Cain mumbled into the soil below him, "Alone? I will be destroyed..."

"No one can destroy you without My vengeance pursuing him. I leave My mark on you to protect you."

Cain dared to look up, out of sheer astonishment, forgetting his fear for a moment.

The Child had become a towering column of light and fire, which, though it burned brightly, consumed nothing.

"I am your God, the God of your father, Adam. Believe, now that you have seen."

Then, in an instant, the column was gone. Cain was left in the heat of the howling wasteland as before. However, new life bloomed in the heart of the man who had been spared.

The venom, the darkness, the hatred, and the frustration were all beaten back, replaced by a cleansing peace that pervaded Cain's senses. Suddenly everything, even the dry barrenness and the wasted grasses around him, seemed a joy and a privilege to be appreciated by a grateful heart.

The soul of the man was exalted with joy, and Cain leapt and laughed with the abandonment of a life cleansed and restored.

He finally stopped, panting and gasping, but rejoicing in his tiredness. He was still alive to experience it! Finally, the unbeliever was clearly able to see where he fit in God's plan and why the world was as it had to be.

For he had seen with new eyes what awaited him after this life, and it was much better than anything he would ever experience here. However, he also knew that this life had to be lived first, in order to obtain the treasures of the next.

His ears picked up a sound of rustling in the dry grasses just over the hill, and he crept up quietly to see where it came from. Clearing the top of the knoll, he was overjoyed to see his herd of goats. Somehowthat they had followed him, or God had seen fit to send them to him. Either way, he was profoundly grateful they were here. They were not only his meat and drink, they were his only companions in the exile he willingly took on.

Behind a stunted tree several yards away was the serpent. It looked on, hissing and writhing in anger. "No! This cannot be!"

"Patience," crooned another voice. A woman's voice, as cool and soothing as a pool of water. She stroked the snake, and it slid up her arm to wrap around her shoulders.

She sat on a boulder, her jet-black hair cascading down her naked back. Her alabaster face was set in a determined line, her coal-black eyes watching the young man cavort with his herd. Opening her blood-red mouth, she ran her tongue over her teeth, and over the fangs as sharp as her companion's. She smiled in a way that would have stopped a man's heart with its evilness. "He will be ours."

Cain danced ahead of his bleating, hungry goats. They needed a place to fill their bellies and a safe place to bed down for the night, and there was nothing in sight.

Isn't it wonderful? he thought. *A test, but God will provide.* Cain knew without a doubt; He would do so, if only for the dumb beasts that followed at their herder's feet.

An odd sound distracted him from his thoughts. A musical sound, light and sweet, came from the withered branches of a dead tree along the path. A small brown bird hopped along a limb, singing its little heart out. Cain had seen many of these creatures near his parents' home, and had killed many just out of boredom. For a moment, his heart was heavy as he replayed those times in his mind.

The bird sang more and more loudly, and then suddenly flew up in a joyous spiral. As Cain watched, smiling and enchanted at the ballet performed by this small delight, the bird flew off toward the setting sun. Cain watched until it disappeared, then turned to continue his journey.

Something else caught his eye—a small patch of green in the distance. Grass. That meant water. *Thank you, God!* He got behind his herd and clapped loudly, and they jumped forward, catching his excitement. Together they rushed toward the oasis Cain had spied.

It was further away than he had reckoned. The sun was almost below the horizon when they finally reached the edge of the greensward. It was much bigger than he had thought also. Trees lush with healthy foliage ringed a grassy plain, with a pool of clean, clear water at the center.

The goats needed no coaxing. They tripped over each other as they hurled themselves towards the water. Cain lost no time in rushing to slake his thirst as well. He fell at the edge and drank thirstily, not even bothering to use his hands to cup the water. So intent was he on relieving his parched throat that he didn't heed his own first rule of herding: watch for predators.

The thought jerked him up, face dripping. He knew water, being as rare as it was, attracted animals of all types. His herd was important; as it survived, so did he. After glancing around, listening for the rustle of the tall grass and the growl or huff that signaled trouble, he felt relieved enough to go back to the business of filling his mouth with the sweet, wonderful, life-giving gift before him.

The approaching footsteps were so quiet that he heard nothing—until she spoke.

"Welcome, Cain. I've been waiting for you."

Cain whirled around and sat up, a rock instantly clutched in his hand and held aloft, ready to be thrown. What he saw before him was so unexpected, so shocking, that the stone tumbled out of his fist onto the ground. He couldn't think of what to say; he could only stare dumbly at the vision before him.

He had never seen a woman besides his mother before. From what he knew or guessed, none others even existed; but here, standing before him, was definitely a woman. The young man was astounded. His eyes traveled over her naked form, unabashedly drinking in her beauty.

His reverie was broken when she gave a low, soft laugh. "Have you never seen a woman before, Cain?" she asked. Her voice was as the music of the morning birds, even as the moon was rising behind her.

Cain blinked, suddenly besotted. "Just my mother, and not...like..." He waved his hand at her form, suddenly peculiarly uncomfortable.

Something in his past, something his parents told him...

His new companion made herself comfortable in the grass beside him. "I am called Lilith."

There was silence; Cain knew of nothing to say in the presence of this quite unexpected company. His gaze went round to his goats, the moon, the trees, anywhere but at Lilith. "How do you know who I am?" he addressed the ground.

"Oh, I have watched you from places where you couldn't see me. I have seen you with your family, and just today I saw you leave them and come towards this place."

Cain suddenly trembled with the memory of what had happened with Abel. Did she know? Had she seen?

He heard her sigh. "Yes, I know about Abel."

Cain's head shot up. How did she know what he had been thinking? So now what? He braced for more admonishment.

"It couldn't be helped, Cain."

What? He stared at her, wide-eyed.

She regarded him with a warm smile. "It's really quite simple. You didn't know what you were doing. Besides, if God had wanted him to live, you would not have been able to kill him, yes?"

Cain gave that statement some thought. True, Abel seemed to have extreme good fortune. And what of all of these...*beings*...helping him build his garden wall? Why did it take so little for him to die?

Then he remembered Abel surrounded by that light. Was he so close to God that He took His beloved to Himself? That warmth and peace. Could he himself be there some day?

"Cain!" Lilith's shout snapped him back to the present. For a mere moment, the look in her eyes terrified him. In the shadows of her face, they looked almost red in appearance.

He shook his head, and met her gaze again. The moment had passed, and the young man wondered if it had ever happened at all.

Lilith lay on her side, propped up on her elbow in the lush grass. Cain felt the stirrings of something within him. It quickly bloomed into a need, which drowned out all else besides the desire to...*what*? He had never had this experience, and did not know how to deal with it.

Lilith did. She drew close, but as she did, Cain's attention was diverted by movement in the foliage behind her.

He gasped and drew away, his eyes locked on the thing creeping out of the bushes. His hand desperately searched for a rock or some other weapon.

A snake! It was huge and black, coming straight toward Lilith. The woman glanced over her shoulder and also saw the reptile. To Cain's surprise, instead of trying to scramble away, she did something that amazed him.

She picked the snake up! It twined itself around her arm and rested its head on her shoulder. Even in the moonlight, its basilisk stare and frozen reptilian smile were distinct and unnerving. "Put down the stone, Cain. This is a...companion...of mine. It won't harm you."

Cain slowly put down his weapon, with a dim memory of snakes and madness. Or was it a dream? He locked eyes with the huge reptile. Its forked tongue flicked out as it regarded him.

After a few minutes, which seemed an eternity to the frightened man, the snake slid off Lilith's shoulder and slithered away into the brush.

Lilith watched it go, a smile very much like her *companion's* on her face. She then turned to Cain. "Come to me."

He did, willingly. In the moonlight, he was again struck by her beauty. Succumbing to her delights, he was totally and blissfully unaware when she sank her fangs into his throat.

CHAPTER 4

Cain woke up, remembering nothing except for his union with Lilith. He lay on his back with his eyes closed, smiling dreamily.

Then, sudden horrid realization hit him. His eyes weren't closed. He was staring into complete darkness.

Panic fired within him as he sat up, looking around wildly for some indication of light, or shadow, or form in this inky blackness. Never in his life had he experienced such a complete void of light. Even on the darkest nights, sleeping outside under the open sky with his family or at the mouth of a cave, there was always enough light to distinguish tree from rock, brush from beast. Even fluttering his fingers close to his eyes brought no indication of sight, merely the movement of air as he waved.

Suddenly he heard a faint sound that brought cold fear to his heart. He could hear his goats bleating wildly and frantically; something was after the herd. He had to go to them. Yet how could he do anything if he couldn't see?

He had to do *something*. These animals were his means of survival, and he couldn't let them just be killed by wild beasts. He had to take some sort of action. Cain crawled towards the sound, cutting his legs and knees on sharp rocks that seemed to be everywhere. As he continued, the sound of the panicked animals became louder, and now he could also hear other sounds. Curious sounds, almost human, which was puzzling. He was not aware of others of his kind anywhere. Well, except for Lilith.

It came to him then that there *were* other people in the world. He had long labored under the impression that his little family was alone in all of Creation. Now, though, he could make out other voices that were unlike any animals he had ever heard.

As he made his laborious way through the dark labyrinth, he noted that forms were beginning to take shape around him. He still couldn't make out any details; they more like darker shapes separating from lighter ones. Cain realized that he'd been in the deepest bowels of a cave, but didn't recall having gone into it.

His charges' insistent, frightened sounds seemed to escalate, and Cain struggled to his feet, preparing to run the rest of the way to save his beasts. A sudden wave of dizziness caught him off-guard, and he fell back onto the ground. Gasping on the rock-strewn floor of the cave, he lay feeling weak and spent, as if he'd run through the desert during mid-day.

Cain felt the slithering body of the serpent, blacker than any of the darkest shadows around it, before he felt the rasp of its scales as it brushed up beside him. He yelled and rolled away from it, only to feel its pulsing body twist around his leg and quickly up to his chest, where it lay staring with fire-red eyes into the powerless man's own. The basilisk glare of the reptile unnerved Cain; he couldn't move or speak.

To his surprise, the snake addressed him in Cain's own language. "Patience. Stay here."

Cain shook his head, breaking their connection, and shifted himself so as to make the creature fall off him. Rather than submit to being unceremoniously dumped from his unwilling host, the serpent picked its head up and, with a slight, graceful movement, returned to the floor of the cave. It merely watched Cain as he decided what to do next.

Cain took the opportunity to once again struggle to his feet, and stumbled unsteadily toward the entrance of the cave. It was still very dim, but he knew he was close. He started walking, then running as his strength returned. Rounding a final corner, he found himself within a few paces of the entrance. What he saw outside first panicked, then enraged him.

Several human-like creatures were throwing stones at Cain's herd, trying to get the goats to move away from near the cave entrance. The poor, frightened animals would simply run, wild-eyed, from one spot to another, never going further than a few yards away. The humans were laughing and calling to each other while they tortured the goats.

With a wild cry, Cain ran out of the cave, waving his arms. He had eyes only for the men haranguing his flock. The strangers' eyes flew open wide when they saw him, and as one, ran from the goats and back over the dunes that ringed the cave. Cain barely had time to savor his victory when a sudden burning sensation shot through him like lightning. He fell on the grass, writhing and screaming.

The sun! It was so hot! Worse than summer at its peak. Cain felt as if his blood was boiling. His skin felt as if it was falling off his bones, and his tongue shriveled up in his mouth. He flung his arm up to shield his eyes against the glare, and gasped at what he saw.

His arm, just yesterday so tanned and strong, was pale white and wrinkled to where he couldn't recognize it as his own. He brought his hand into his vision, and almost screamed.

There was a claw-like appendage where his hand had been. It was certainly the same hand he'd always had, but his fingers had curled with the heat of the sun, and his fingernails had become long, sharp claws! The sight, along with the sunlight and heat, were too much for him, and he passed out.

An eternity later, or so it seemed, Cain once again woke to darkness, but not the complete lack of light he had experienced earlier. He could see the stars outside the mouth of the cave, and felt the coolness of the evening breeze on his face. Gradually, he grew aware of another presence.

Her presence.

Turning his head, he could see her sitting a short distance away, watching him. A smile played across her lips, fully forming as he sat up.

"Ah, you're awake."

Cain rubbed his eyes with the palms of his hands, and was once again shocked at what he saw. His skin, muscle, and sinew were back to their tanned, well-proportioned shapes. How, though, and what happened earlier to have caused their change to that awful condition?

"So many questions."

Her statement was spoken so quietly that Cain almost thought he'd imagined he'd heard her speak. Lilith came closer, lying down on the ground beside him. He pulled away slightly, the germ of a disconcerting thought stirring in his mind. "You are confused. Let me help clear up whatever questions you have."

One look into those soft, sweet eyes took away all of Cain's will and resistance. He smiled back, relaxing. "I do have some questions. Like how I ended up in here, and why the sun hurt me so bad when I went out to protect my goats...?"

He suddenly realized that he wasn't hearing the usual snorts and hoof shuffling of his herd as they grazed. Were they all gone? This couldn't be; he'd starve without them. Cain leapt to his feet and ran outside into the night.

No goats.

He fought the sand dunes until he was on top of them, and looked frantically across the plains and hillsides as far as he could see. They were gone.

Despondent, he slid back down the dune the way he had gone up. His shoulders slumped, and he mentally prepared for death. No goats meant no milk or meat. Without that, in this harsh environment, he would starve within days.

Lilith was still where she was when he'd bolted out of the cave. Not alone, though; the serpent was with her once again. They waited expectantly as he slowly walked towards them. He slumped down onto a boulder and put his head in his hands.

A small bleat made him rear up and look at Lilith. She had a small kid goat in her arms, and was stroking its head. Regarding Cain with gentleness, she said, "Some are still here. Many are gone, taken by those men you saw earlier."

She looked at him sharply. "You did not know there were others like you, did you? Something no one bothered to tell you. There are many other men near, as well as women and children."

Cain was interested. Women? He could have his own mate and family? They'd probably have plenty of food and water, and there would be many people to speak to. "Where are they?" he demanded. "I have to go to them."

"Soon. We will all go." As she said this, the serpent curled itself around her shoulders.

It spoke. "Yes, we will go meet these people."

"And I would like to stay with them, and live with them." Cain had made up his mind.

Lilith's smile changed almost unperceptively, but just for a moment. However, something he saw in that brief change terrified Cain, a feeling that took a long time to dissipate after her smile returned to the soft, sensuous one he had become used to. What it was that shook him, he did not know.

"You will certainly meet them. As time passes, you will be drawn to them." Lilith's eyes hardened as her gaze bored into Cain, "but you will live with us. I want to have you as my mate."

Cain's jaw dropped. "Me?"

"Oh, yes. We will spend eternity together. I decided this a long time ago, as I watched you grow up."

Cain blinked. She couldn't be any older than he was, so how could she have seen him in his childhood?

"There are many questions that I can answer for you. Just stay here with me, and I will teach you everything." This was not Lilith speaking, although it seemed it was at first. The voice, deep and rich, resonated from the serpent. The sound filled Cain's ears, penetrated his mind, and took over his very being. He felt caught up in it, as if the voice had a life of its own within him. As the snake twisted itself around Lilith's shoulders, its voice twined throughout Cain's thoughts and around his heart, rendering him impervious to any other influences, physical or spiritual. He locked himself onto the serpent's command and floated unyielding into its power.

In this dreamlike state, he looked back to Lilith. She was doing something with the kid goat. Cain squinted in the darkness, and watched emotionlessly as she brought the creature's head up, exposing its neck. She looked up at Cain, locking his eyes in a hypnotic gaze.

The moon had risen, and the light shone on Lilith and the goat. It was such a peaceful scene; Cain didn't realize Lilith was so fond of the little animal. Then Lilith smiled widely, exposing her fangs. She opened her mouth wide, and struck the goat hard. It shrieked, struggled, then was still as she drained it of its life.

Cain's hand flew to his own throat, feeling for the first time the holes in his skin—holes that had not been there before his first encounter with Lilith. Reality hit him, and, shocked at what had happened, he jumped to his feet. As he attempted to run away, he was paralyzed by a heaviness around his ankle. Looking down, he was terrified to see the serpent twining itself around his leg. It spoke again; Cain tried to block it out, but he was powerless to do so. "You do not really want to leave. For you are mine. I lost the fight for your parents, but I will not lose you."

With cold fear clutching his heart, Cain now understood—this was no ordinary reptile. It was the one his parents had told him about, the one in the garden. The one that had tempted his mother. The one that had gotten them thrown out into this horrid exile.

As much as he struggled, he was rooted to the spot. The snake's weight had become tremendous, and Cain could not shift its weight. It smiled as Lilith drew close with the goat.

She held the little body towards him. Cain gasped as he saw her red mouth, the goat's blood dripping down her chin. "Drink."

Cain stared aghast at the dead creature held out to him. Blood pooled as it burbled slowly out of the two holes where Lilith had bitten through fur, skin and vein to slake her own unnatural thirst. He shook violently, screamed, and tried to push her away.

Then another sensation took over. His throat suddenly felt parched, and he realized he had had nothing to eat or drink since Lilith had found him at the oasis. He looked at the carcass...No! This was wrong!

"You wanted strength, Cain," the snake purred as it rose, twisting, to above the man's waist. "An animal's strength is in its blood. Without it, as you see, it dies. You will not be able to draw its strength by any other means."

"No! I can't! I won't!" Cain tried to break away again, without success.

Suddenly the reptile was eye-to-eye with Cain. Its eyes, burning red, stared directly into its victim's mind. "You will."

Something happened within Cain's conscience, a struggle he felt distantly, as if it was happening to someone else. He began having a series of visions. The first was one of a small child with golden hair. Cain reached out and grasped the child by the throat, tearing it open with one stroke. As the Child died, Cain could see His blood flowing, not from His throat, but from a myriad of wounds everywhere on His body. Most notable were large, heavily bleeding holes on the Boy's hands and feet.

Cain looked at his own hands, confused. He knew he hadn't done that. How did it happen?

The Child disappeared, and Abel took His place. He looked alarmed, and held his arms out pleadingly to Cain. It seemed he was trying to say something, but Cain couldn't hear him.

The Child appeared beside Abel, unblemished except for the odd wounds in His hands and feet. Standing next to Abel, he looked at Cain, disappointment and sadness in His eyes. Then He touched Abel's arm, and together they turned and walked slowly away. Soon they disappeared.

"Follow, Cain." The voice, gentle and sad, echoed in Cain's mind. He stepped forward, wanting to follow his brother.

A squeezing on his throat blocked his breathing, shocking him out of his dream state, while at the same time he felt something salty, warm, and bitter pass through his lips. Sudden sharp focus made him realize what was happening.

Lilith had the goat's throat up to Cain's lips, pressing it against them. Instead of being repulsed, an irresistible urge overtook him, and he fell without reservation into feeding. The craving for blood filled his mind and body; he grabbed the goat from Lilith and sucked greedily, squeezing the small body to find even more that had not yet been drawn from it.

Lilith forcibly took the carcass away as Cain continued to pull at the animal's throat. She finally got it away from him and tossed it to the ground. Cain stared hungrily at the pile of fur and bones. His eyes were wild with a blood lust, and only the weight of the serpent kept him from falling on it to resume feeding.

Lilith touched his arm. "Come, let us visit the people we saw earlier."

Cain was astounded. It was night. All would be asleep. Why now? He found himself following her willingly, knowing that staying with Lilith meant being able to slake his blood-thirst and grow more powerful.

They made their way towards a grouping of fires in the distance. As they got closer, Cain could see sleeping forms around the family hearths. A few stirred in their sleep, and one or two cried out in their dreams. The two visitors crouched down behind a large boulder. Lilith seemed to be waiting for something.

Suddenly she pointed. Cain could see someone moving. A man had gotten up and was walking away from his hearth. As he walked into the darkness outside the safety of the hearth fires' light, Lilith tensed. "Watch and learn," she whispered, gesturing to Cain to stay where he was.

He watched as she leapt noiselessly out from behind the boulder as the man passed by. She jumped onto his back, driving her knees into his spine while she pulled his head back, breaking his neck. As he went down, she bit into his neck as she had with the goat.

While she fed, she gestured to Cain to come to her. He walked over as if in a dream, and offered no resistance as she pushed his mouth to the throat of the poor wretch who had made the wrong choice at the wrong time. Cain pulled and pulled, the sticky, hot blood filling his own being with power and strength. He knew then that he was unable to resist anymore.

What's more, he didn't want to.

A short distance away, the serpent laughed softly to itself as it watched.

CHAPTER 5

Darkness again met Cain's eyes when he awoke. He blinked as he looked around, trying to discern shapes in the black void. From the damp smell, he knew he was back in the cave. The sound of water trickling down the wall of the cavern came to his ears.

An incredible thirst suddenly overwhelmed him. Feeling his way, he crawled toward the sound, until he could feel the water running over his hands. Without hesitation, Cain thrust his head into the stream, drinking like one of his goats. As he drank, a peculiar sensation crept into his subconscious. It finally became so strong that he had to stop what he was doing.

What was it? *Why am I feeling so odd?*

Then it dawned on him: The water...burned? Although it was cold to the touch, it stung his mouth and throat. Not so much that it was painful, just...uncomfortable.

Strange. He sat back, staring towards the sound of the rivulet as it trickled and dripped.

It didn't make sense. None of this made sense.

Cain remembered nothing of what had happened the previous night. It was as if a hand had somehow wiped away the memory of his visit to the other humans. He moved toward what he hoped was the mouth of the cave. After a few minutes of searching, he realized he was seeing the palest of light ahead of him.

He soon came to the entrance. The serpent and the woman didn't seem to be around, for which he was grateful.

Why? Aren't they my only friends? Again, something had changed. A thought had begun stirring in his mind; it had probably begun before he'd even awakened. Maybe they weren't what they seemed to be...*but why am I thinking this way?*

Cain looked out at the evening sky. The sun had just disappeared beyond the horizon, and faint stars were beginning to appear. All was peaceful. He took a deep breath, inhaling the dusty, heat-soaked air, now beginning to cool with the oncoming night. This had always been his favorite time of day. Perfect for herding his goats or resting under a tree.

My goats! Cain remembered with a panicked jolt. *Where are my goats?*

He ran out across the desert, tripping over grasses and rocks as he squinted into the darkening distance for their shapes.

Those men. They have them. He had to get them back, had to get out of here. Away from Lilith, back to his parents. He was in an all-out panic as he ran headlong to where he thought the tribe of strangers was camped. A faint bleating noise caused him to stop and listen.

Yes! There it was again, under those trees.

Cain moved forward again, a little more stealthily this time, in case the men were with the goats. As he drew close, he realized that the herd was in a hollow, under the stand of trees. He moved quietly to where the ground rose up and, lying down, peered over the top of the rise.

There they were! Well, it was a herd of goats; whether or not they were his was impossible to tell. He did not see any goatherds about, so who would know if he took them away?

Suddenly Cain's neck hairs stiffened. He knew he wasn't alone.

A low growl alerted him to the presence of a small, four-footed predator not too far from him. Intent on the herd, it didn't pay attention to the man lying upwind of it. As it tensed its shoulders, preparing to attack, so did Cain; but his quarry was the predator. His first thought had been to protect the animals grazing peacefully below, but another sensation soon overtook that one—he wanted the predator's life. Its blood.

With movements faster than he thought possible, Cain was on the animal, his hands around its throat, his knee on its back. It took very little effort to break the creature's spine.

Sometime during the past few minutes, Cain's fingers had once again become claws. He was grateful this time; he slashed the beast's jugular vein open with them, and began devouring the blood that spurted forth.

Again, the uncanny, overwhelming feeling of power. The red mist before his eyes. The loss of all sensation, except for the hot, salty life force pouring into him from the creature under his control. When he could no longer draw life from the animal, Cain fell back, panting. He lay on the side of the low hill, staring up at the night sky.

Soft shuffling at the foot of the hill caused him to turn his head, curious as to what was approaching, with the vague notion that perhaps here was another meal. To his utter surprise, a young girl stood amid the goats, staring up at him. The herd was milling around, uncomfortable at the smell of death. Their bleating had reached the girl's ears, and she had run to see what the commotion was about.

Cain sat up quickly, wiping the blood from his mouth. The girl looked on the verge of panic herself, and no wonder. Here was a complete stranger, lying near her goats, smeared with blood.

Then her eyes slid to the carcass of the predator, lying still and cold next to him. The panic left her eyes, and she smiled at him.

"Thank you for protecting my goats," she said to Cain.

Another surprise; she spoke the same kinds of words as he did. Although why he should expect otherwise, he did not know. He was expecting grunts or other animal sounds. This was a pleasant revelation.

Hesitatingly, he nodded his head. He didn't know what to say.

She took a step forward, and Cain moved back, his hands behind him so they wouldn't frighten her. For some reason, he didn't trust himself being near her. Faint memories—*a man in the dark, he and Lilith hiding—why?* There was a reason, but he couldn't quite grasp it.

"Where are your people?" asked the girl.

He finally found his voice. "A long ways from here. Towards where the sun went down. I don't really know anymore."

"Come with me to my family's hearth. My people will be happy to learn of what you did tonight."

CHAPTER 6

Cain stumbled along behind the girl, as mute and mindless as one of his own goats. Only her faint outline in the gathering night kept him moving in the right direction.

The young woman spoke again. "I am called Naya. What are you called?"

"Umm...Cain."

Naya smiled over her shoulder at him.

"Please, walk beside me. It's hard to talk to you when you are behind me."

Cain wasn't too sure he wanted to get that close. The taste of blood was still in his mouth, and he was wanting more. His breathing became labored as he moved closer to Naya, his claws outstretched to take her.

But, wait...

He stared at his hands, now reverted back to their human shape. Naya turned at that moment and, seeing his hands outstretched, grasped them with her own. "Is it too dark to find your way? Here, let me help you."

My way? What way? Cain couldn't think. All he was aware of was her small hands in his.

She was pulling him along to where he could see a fire blazing in the distance. He could make out several people around it, and little ones scampering about in the dust surrounding the hearths. He could hear their playful cries and shouts as he and Naya approached the camp.

An odd smell reached his nostrils, and he could see that they were sharing a meal of some sort. They were taking it from something that was over the fire. The odor was one he'd never smelled before, but it was intoxicating; he found that his mouth was watering. Gone was the thirst for blood, and in its place was true hunger, and a wish to share in what these people were eating. He hoped they'd offer him some of whatever it was; it hit him with a jolt that he couldn't remember having eaten anything in at least a day, if not more.

The party at the hearth turned at the sound of Naya and Cain approaching. The brightness of the fire made it impossible for the group to see who was coming towards them; two of the younger men jumped up, rocks in their fists, and snarled a warning.

"Tibek! Itzeh! It is just me, Naya. And I've found...someone."

Naya pushed Cain forward into the light. He shuddered pleasantly as she held his arm and smiled broadly at her family. Cain hoped that his face was cleared of blood; he smiled uncertainly, lips twitching. If he still had fangs, he didn't want them to know. His gaze jumped from one face to another; from the stony stare of an older man, still seated, to the defensive glares of the two young men, to the frightened eyes of several women huddling together on the far side of the fire. The children stopped their play, standing as still as the rocks they had been clambering on. No one spoke.

Finally, with a grunt, the older man stood up. He waved off one of the women who had run up to help him. At a sign from him, the two younger men stepped back, arms lowered, but with the rocks still gripped tightly.

"Naya, what is this? Why have you brought this man here? We do not know him, or his clan."

"Father, I found him with the goats. He had killed a wild beast that had threatened the herd."

"Where was Jopa? Why is he not watching the goats?"

Naya shook her head. "I don't know. I guess he had...something...he had to do. All I know is, I was on my way to see if Jopa needed anything, and when I heard the goats crying out, I ran to them. I did not see Jopa, just this man, Cain, and a dead jackal."

The elder glanced at the two armed men. "Go to the herd. Find Jopa."

They moved out into the dark. Cain swallowed hard as the older man turned his gaze back to him. Sweat popped out on the younger man's forehead, and he shuffled his feet uncomfortably as he tried to outstare the elder.

The silence was deafening as the two men's gazes remained locked, each trying to attain dominance; the elder, because it was his right as the head of the clan, and Cain because he instinctively felt that he had to prove his strength to these strangers. He wasn't about to back down, or they would throw him out into the night.

Naya, for her part, became more and more nervous, glancing back and forth between the two men. "Father! Please! Say something!" she finally blurted out. An older woman shushed her and pulled her toward the huddled women.

"Mother!" Naya pulled away. "Cain is a good man!" She stomped her foot and turned her back to the clan, crossed her arms, and glared out into the darkness.

The tension was broken by the two men running back into the light cast by the fire. For a moment, they couldn't speak as they gasped for breath. "Jopa...," gasped out the taller of the two, "he's...he's...his...," he gestured toward his own throat, "...torn..."

Naya's father closed his eyes and nodded, as if he had been expecting such news. Cain hoped against hope that Jopa had not been one of his victims, and then wondered with shock why he would have even thought of such a thing. Memories of the last couple of days and nights were fading...

With a speed unexpected from someone his advanced age, Naya's father sprang on Cain, grabbing the hair on the back of the young man's head and pulling back. Cain fell to his knees, crying out in pain.

"What did you do to Jopa?" he demanded, fury blazing in his eyes.

The two scouts cried out, pulling the older man off of the poor stranger. They had more to reveal.

"Father! No! We saw it happen!" the younger of the two shouted.

The elder stood back, flanked by his sons, breathing hard. He glanced at the two. Cain remained on the ground, too frightened to move, but listening with interest. "What do you mean?" the old man growled.

"We got to the herd, and saw Jopa sitting on a rock, keeping watch. As we approached and were about to call out, a huge black snake came out of nowhere and raced up his body. It went so fast, and it struck him as it coiled up around his neck. It...tore him...choked him...we tried to get it off, but we couldn't..." His voice trailed off as he started to sob.

The women, their terror mounting as they heard the tale, wailed their grief and moved as one to the men. Naya stood, shaking, alone to one side. The children clung to their mothers' legs, bewildered as to why everyone was upset.

Cain stood and walked to Naya. He put his arm around her, and she collapsed against him, sobbing. He stood looking out at the night and thinking. *The serpent...* His eyes narrowed as he tried to remember details about that creature.

Wasn't it supposed to be my friend? Or...was it?

He suddenly realized with terrible clarity: that snake was trying to destroy him. It had followed him here, and had killed Jopa instead of him. Was that a mistake...or a warning? The realization shook him. His decision was made in an instant.

No more. His life was to be with these people. This was where he belonged, not in some dream world with a strange woman and her pet. Cain gave Naya another reassuring hug, then released her and walked to the rest of her sobbing family. He put his hand on the grieving father's shoulder. "I am sorry about Jopa. And now the goats are out there alone. Someone must go and watch over them. Let me do that for you. I...I herded goats for my clan before I left."

The elder looked at Cain in a daze of hurt and pain. Working through his emotion, he finally nodded. Then he looked over at Naya. "Go with him. Take turns sleeping. We need these goats. They are our lives."

He gave Cain a long look. "Let me know if this one takes them and deserts us." He then gestured to Tibek to follow them.

Cain nodded once, ignoring the barb. He and Naya stepped out into the night.

Early the next morning, just before sunrise, Cain woke to find Naya slumbering beside him. The goats were ranged comfortably around them, unharmed through the dark hours. Tibek was nowhere in sight. Cain assumed he had returned to the hearth, satisfied of the newcomer's honesty.

Suddenly, something made Cain uneasy. He peered into the distance, then looked quickly behind the tree under which they were lying. Nothing...*but something*... A light laugh came from above him. He looked up and gasped.

Lilith! There she was, perched on a high limb. The serpent was coiled loosely around her, its head in its usual place on her shoulder. She smiled seductively. Unbidden, the memory of his time with her came back, and he recoiled with horror as he remembered...everything...

"Cain, my dear boy," purred Lilith, "what are you doing here?"

"Quiet! Don't wake her," Cain hissed. He glanced down at Naya's sleeping form, then back up to Lilith. She gazed at Naya with mild interest, running her tongue over her lips. She laughed low in her throat. "Why are you here?"

he whispered, looking up at the woman sliding along the branch towards him. He trembled, fearful at the answer.

"I've come to bring you back, of course."

Cain looked away, his resolve of the night before being shaken under her hypnotic stare.

"No!" he managed to get out. "I am staying here. These are my people." He dared a glance up at her again.

Lilith hissed, her fangs glinting in the pre-dawn light emanating from where the sun was about to peek over the horizon. Cain almost screamed at the sight, and he remembered that he, too, had had such teeth not all that long ago.

He staggered away from Naya, from the tree, into the desert. His head swam, his stomach knotted. Through the buzzing in his anguished mind came an evil laugh, and Lilith's voice. "Yes, Cain, remember. Remember that you are no longer one of them. You cannot live among them. You belong to us now. Look, Cain. The sun is coming up."

Cain squinted at the sunrise. He could feel it burning his skin, could feel the talons returning to his hands, the sharpness of the fangs within his mouth. He cried out in pain, and in something more visceral. A voice he didn't recognize tore itself, unbidden, from his very core. "My God, have mercy on me!"

The sound echoed across the flat, dry plains and called back from the hills. Cain fell to his knees, astonished and terror-stricken. A shriek emanated from the tree, as Lilith vanished in a mass of oily black smoke. The serpent froze for a moment, then, its eyes intent on the form below it, slithered down the trunk. It paused at Naya's head, and bared its own fangs. A deep, growling voice echoed in Cain's mind:

"This is not over, mortal." It reared as if to strike, but at the last moment, it turned abruptly and slithered away into the tall grass.

CHAPTER 7

Cain was numb. He couldn't move, couldn't speak; he could only stare, paralyzed, in the direction the serpent had gone. Gradually, he became aware of his surroundings again—the sound of birdsong, the warmth of the rising sun on his back...

The sun!

While just a few moments ago it had been burning his skin, the light was now merely a gentle radiance. Instead of making him want to scurry into the dark like a rat, he could face it again as he always had before.

Before Lilith.

Before the Serpent.

Before the evil that had enveloped and taken over his soul.

Once again, he was redeemed. Free.

Cain fell forward, sobbing and laughing in turn. He rolled in the sand and dry grass, luxuriating in the relief that came from being once again forgiven and liberated from the grasp of evil.

Yet another chance. This time he would not go back.

He lay on his back, eyes closed, basking in the sunlight. Content for the first time in days, he stayed still, letting the warmth permeate his entire being.

A small cry caught his attention. Naya!

He sat up and looked over at her. The poor girl was sitting upright under the tree, staring at him wide-eyed. Her knees were tucked up under her chin; she looked as if she was trying to make herself invisible. The grass behind her rustled, and she shrieked, rolling away from the sound. A kid goat parted the growth. Relieved, Naya crawled to it, gratefully putting her arms around its neck. She buried her face in the startled animal's coat.

Cain got up off the ground and walked back to Naya. As he approached, he could see that she was shaking with fear. He hurried to her, dropping to his knees by her side. "Naya? What is wrong?"

She stared up at him, and the terror could be plainly seen on her face. "Didn't you see that snake? I have never seen one so big, and so black. And it almost bit me! What if..." Her eyes widened with the realization. "Yes, that is probably the same snake that killed Jopa." She looked back at the grass, thoughtful for a moment. The goat struggled in her arms, and she let it go. Then she looked up again at Cain.

"But—it didn't. It looked out at you, and it looked...scared? Then it left." A new respect replaced wonder as she gazed at him. "What did you do?" she asked quietly.

It was Cain's turn to be startled. "Me?" He thought quickly. She had obviously slept through the morning's events, up until she woke to find the snake poised over her. It was fortunate, for both of them, that she had done so. It was much easier to explain this way.

He shook his head, smiling gently. "Come. Let us go back to your family's hearth. I can tell you while we walk."

On the trail from the herd to the camp, Cain told her, "It wasn't me who scared away the snake. It was the work of the Creator."

Naya looked puzzled. "'Creator'? What is that?"

Another surprise. Cain looked over at Naya in astonishment. She innocently stared back, waiting expectantly for an answer. "You mean you've never heard of the Creator? God? The One who made all of us, and," he swept his arm, indicating their surroundings, "all of this?"

Naya shook her head. "I have never heard of this Creator. What is it?"

Cain rubbed his face. This would not be as easy as he first thought. He tried a different approach. "Don't you wonder where all this came from? Where you came from? How you happened to be here? Someone beyond this world had to have created it."

Naya gave Cain's words some thought. Then she shook her head again. "What we know is, we are...Here...and then we are...Gone. And that is true of everything we see. There is nothing else."

Cain opened his mouth to explain further, but was unable to come up with an answer he thought she could understand. Fortunately, Naya was distracted by the approach of several clan members. Cain recognized Naya's parents, and several sisters. The men, Tibek and Itzeh, were back at the camp, tending something over the fire. There were several other men there also, working over the carcass of a large animal.

The entourage was accompanied by several of the little children, who scampered and ran around them. Always playing, always innocent. Cain wished he was one of them, rather than the outsider being judged.

Naya's father, walking ahead of the small envoy, stopped abruptly. Everyone else, except for the little ones, stopped as well. The adults all stared warily at Cain. For several long moments, no one spoke. Except for the droning of insects and the distant bleating of the herd, all was silent.

The elder spoke, his frosty glare focused on the young man next to his daughter, her arm in his. "So. Did anything else get slaughtered in the night?"

Naya's mother put a hand on her mate's arm. "Enoch..." she chided him reprovingly.

He growled at her, and she stepped back. "Nesa," he threw back over his shoulder, "I do not trust this Cain."

"Father, please," Naya looked imploringly at Enoch. "This morning he saved my life."

Enoch's glare thawed a bit, but the hostility remained. "Tell me."

"I was sleeping, and I woke up, and there was this huge serpent right by my head. Father, I'm sure it's the one that killed Jopa."

The women behind Enoch gasped. He merely flicked a glance at Naya before returning his stare to Cain. This time, there was some interest in his eyes.

Cain noticed the younger women scattering to pull the children in, all the while glancing around worriedly for serpentine forms hiding in the shadows.

"Go on." Enoch folded his arms.

"I don't know what Cain did, but suddenly the snake looked at him and...left."

"Hmph. And he didn't go after it, to kill it?"

Cain stared back at the old man. This was unreasonable. *What did he expect?* Then again, Enoch had no idea who that Serpent was, so Cain couldn't really blame him for his ignorance. And he wasn't about to try to explain. Too many layers, none of which would be understandable to a people who had no belief in the God of Adam and Eve.

He decided to use the easiest route. Smiling at Enoch, he said, "I chased the snake away. It won't return to harm any of us."

A collective sigh of relief went up behind Enoch. He turned and gave them an exasperated look. Then he planted his not-quite-as-cold stare back onto the young man who had suddenly risen to hero status among his womenfolk.

Nesa cleared her throat, and Enoch rolled his eyes, emitting a sigh of his own. He looked back at her. She stepped forward, new respect for Cain in her eyes, and determination in her voice. Looking back and forth between Cain and Enoch, she declared, "I believe him. And I have never had a reason to not believe Naya. I wish for Cain to join us."

Enoch flashed her a look, but its sternness was tempered with love and kindness for the woman he had lived with for so long. "What is this? My mate is deciding this clan's future?"

Cain's heart leaped. He looked down at Naya. She was grinning from ear to ear, practically jumping up and down, watching her parents' faces.

Could it be? Were they going to accept me? His pulse pounded in his ears as he awaited the outcome. Was that what he, himself, wanted? It didn't take him any time to decide that answer.

It was YES!

Enoch looked back at Cain, stern but accepting. "My mate has decided, and I will let her have her way. This once..." He shot a glance at Nesa, who smiled complacently. He rolled his eyes, sighed, and turned again to Cain. "She wishes you to join us," he said in a barely audible voice. Nesa cleared her throat, and Enoch's eyes threw thunderbolts at her. "Yes? What now?"

Nesa gave him a look loaded with meaning, and glanced at Naya. Enoch's eyebrows rose in surprise, and the women around Nesa glanced at each other, excitement dawning on their faces. Several of them were now smiling and whispering behind their hands, throwing looks of their own at Cain and Naya.

Cain felt his face redden. *What was this about?*

Enoch closed his eyes for a moment, sighing. "I knew it would come to this," he muttered to himself.

He opened them and walked towards the young couple. Taking their hands, he grasped them in his own. Cain tried to pull away, uncertain, but Enoch's grip was strong. The elder pulled hard on Cain's arm, then, giving him a sharp look, brought the two younger peoples' hands together.

After an awkward couple of moments, he nudged Cain. "So take her hand," he said gruffly, staring at him under lowered eyebrows.

Cain took it.

"Naya is your mate," Enoch said with some reservation. "It is her...ow!"

Nesa poked him hard.

"*Our* wish that you stay with us. Bring forth many children to ensure our family's survival." He finished speaking and turned away, walking back to the hearth. The rest of them heard him muttering to himself. Most of it was indiscernible, but they caught his last remark:

"Can we get something to eat now?"

Naya squealed with delight, grasping Cain's hand with both of her own. She smiled happily up at him. "Oh, Cain! We are mated!"

She pulled him along behind her, chattering away about their good fortune. Cain, for his part, was once again surprised into mute silence. This was hardly what he had been expecting.

But why not? It means a future, and a family, and living out a normal life with normal people. Plus, a mate of his own also meant...

A small smile played across his lips. Then it broke out into a full-fledged grin as he realized other aspects of having a woman beside him. Especially when it came to sleeping arrangements...

By the time they reached the encampment, Cain was walking beside Naya. They had their arms around each other, walking very close and whispering. The smell of roasting meat wafted to them from the fire pit, and Cain's mouth watered. His stomach rumbled.

"I hope there is something left for your hungry belly, slow one," Naya laughed, breaking into a run.

Laughing, the newly-mated couple raced to where the menfolk were just pulling the meat out of the fire. Everyone waited with respect while Enoch and Nesa took their portion, then they all fell upon the remains.

Cain ate his fill of the first cooked meat he had ever tasted. It was wonderful. He couldn't remember when he had had a better meal.

Everyone around him laughed and talked, filling the air with happy sounds. Cain looked around at them, feeling a respect and belonging he had never known.

His people. Yes.

CHAPTER 8

Cain stepped back, watching as the newest arrival to the flock was licked clean by its mother. It never ceased to fascinate him, this process of birthing. In just a short time, a new life where there hadn't been one before. His thoughts traveled back to the day his own first-born had come into the world.

He had gone out to tend the herd as usual. His brothers ran to him soon after, shouting to him that Naya was giving birth. He stood as still as a boulder, not quite grasping what he had just been told. His favorite brother, Pesah, shoved him towards the encampment, grinning.

"Go, father-man. I'll stay here with the animals. Naya needs you."

Cain nodded dazedly and started off slowly in the direction of the hearth. Then it finally caught in his mind. His mate was...

"Oh!!" He broke into a run, oblivious to the cheers of Pesah and the rest of the young men.

How he hoped the child would be a boy. He had already decided that Naya's younger sister's baby girl would be his own child's mate when they came of age.

Ever since Naya's father had Gone, several summers ago, Cain had become the unofficial elder of the clan. Certainly there were other men who could have taken on this role, especially Naya's older brothers, but they were all in awe of his skills with the goats, and his ability to get along well with the nomadic clans that came through their area.

What garnered their respect more than anything else was the idea that Cain had scared away the serpent that had tried to kill Naya. Ever since that day, no one had seen it, and the attacks had stopped. He let them believe the story, because it gave him prestige, and also because it was easier for him to blend into their beliefs rather than to explain what had actually happened. Explaining God's existence didn't seem to be all that important. He found it a relief to just "be", rather than to commit to any kind of fealty to his Creator. Certainly it didn't feel completely right to deny it either, but it would have to do until he could think of some other way to get back to that relationship. He was far too busy to do that right now.

Several of his sisters ran to him as he entered the circle of new shelters that defined the clan's territory. "Naya is having the baby!" they shouted excitedly.

"Yes, Pesah told me." He tried to go past them, but they became a living wall.

"No, you must wait. Mother is with her. You can go in once the baby is born."

A wailing sound came from his shelter. Cain put a hand on a sister's shoulder, and stared into her eyes. It was a look of kindness, but also one of quiet determination. "Rana, I must go to her. I promised I would. Do not keep me from her."

Rana stared back, then dropped her gaze. She moved aside unwillingly. "This just isn't done," he heard her say as he pushed gently past her.

Nesa looked up from her sweating, writhing daughter as Cain entered. At her tired and annoyed expression, he nodded, smiling gently. "Yes, I know. 'Not done'. I heard it from my sisters." He sat down beside her, grasping Naya's hand and looking at his mate's pain-filled face. She squeezed his hand as another contraction tore through her. Her back arched and she screamed. "I had to be here," Cain said to Nesa.

"I know. Most of these men wouldn't do such a thing, but you have always been different somehow."

"I have seen births before. If I can watch and help an animal with birthing..." here he stopped as Naya once again screwed up her face in pain, pushing against the new life demanding to be born, "if I can face that, I have no excuse to not be here for Naya."

Nesa had stopped listening. She was busy with something near Naya's knees, and suddenly there was another cry. Not Naya. Not Nesa. It was the cry of his own child! He sat back, breathless.

Nesa, smiling, held up the struggling, red-faced little mite. "It's a boy. You have a son."

Cain laughed, taking the tiny child to himself. He stared at the little face, the hands clenching into fists. *Such a perfect little boy. And already a fighter.*

Naya held out her arms, and Cain gave her the baby. She laid the little one on her chest, trying to clean him off.

Nesa plucked the child off his mother and, with the experience of one who had done this many times, quickly cleaned him off. She folded him into a fresh goatskin, then handed him back to her daughter. He found her milk supply almost immediately.

Naya looked up at Cain, the ordeal of giving birth showing plainly on her exhausted face. "We shall name him Enoch, after Father."

Cain nodded. It seemed appropriate. After all, the elder Enoch had also seemed always ready for a fight.

Yes, that was a wonderful thing, to see the birth of his son. That was four summers ago, and Enoch was growing into a fine, strong boy. Cain often brought him out to the flock, especially when Naya was feeling ill. This new pregnancy made her very tired. Enoch was so active, and he needed some diversion. Besides, it was never too early to learn herding skills. Today, however, he was home, running with his friends. Cain hoped he was staying out of trouble.

Suddenly a scream rent the twilight. Cain jerked his head towards the hearth.

Naya! Is she in labor? It's too early. No, it doesn't sound like that.

Several of his sisters had had babies since Enoch was born, so he knew the cries and wails that accompanied birth. No, this sounded...scared?

He started running towards his shelter. As he neared the hearth, he looked for movement—people running, or shouting, or something. All was still. There was no movement in the camp. *Where is everyone?*

Then he saw them. His whole clan huddled together beside the entrance to his tent. They seemed to be paralyzed by something they were staring at in front of them. There was movement inside; he could see shapes and hear voices.

And a deep growling...

He knew that sound, and his blood turned to ice. The Serpent was in front of Cain's shelter, hissing and writhing in a death dance that kept everyone mesmerized. He felt himself being drawn into the intoxicating embrace...

"No! Leave Enoch alone!" screamed Naya from inside.

That startled Cain out of the hypnotic trance. He bolted into the shelter, knowing full well who was waiting inside.

The Serpent followed him at a leisurely pace.

Lilith stood by the beds with Enoch in her grasp. Her fire-red eyes bored into the new arrival. "Cain."

Enoch struggled beneath Lilith's talons, holding out his little arms to his father. "Abba!"

Naya lunged at Lilith, screaming. The Serpent struck her full in the chest, and she fell backwards. The black horror wrapped itself around her throat, looking back triumphantly at Cain. It squeezed its body muscles menacingly.

Lilith's eyes slid sideways as she glanced at her companion, then back to Cain.

"No! Let them go!" Cain cried desperately. He looked around for a weapon, knowing that there was no defense against them, but he wouldn't just take this invasion without a fight.

"Oh, we can't do that." Lilith's cold voice chilled him to the bone. "Not without getting what we came for."

Cain, frantic, looked from his son to his mate. Lilith's vicious claws were holding one down, and the other was being slowly strangled to death by the Serpent. He suddenly heard a noise behind him; the trance broken, his brothers had come in, clubs and stones at the ready.

The Serpent increased its stranglehold at the sight of the group of men. Naya's eyes bulged as she struggled to breathe.

Cain screamed at his brothers, "No! Please leave! That snake will kill her!"

"So what happened to your snake-scaring abilities, O Man of Great Achievements?" said the Serpent tauntingly. The snarl emanated through Cain's mind.

"What do you want?" Cain pleaded. Naya kicked out, trying to tear the loathsome coils off her throat. Enoch screamed as Lilith's nails dug into his skin. Drops of blood appeared as she slowly tore into him.

Lilith's eyes grew large, and she opened her fanged mouth. Enoch looked up and cried out in terror. The she-demon drew the boy up, pulling his head back, gazing lustfully at his throat.

"No! Oh God, no! Not Enoch!"

Lilith and the Serpent both flinched at the Name. The snake released its hold, and Naya gulped air. Lilith stopped just as her fangs scratched Enoch's neck.

She looked down and, with an evil smile, licked the blood that seeped out of the wounds.

Cain's stomach churned. He held out his hands, pleading. "Leave them. Please! Don't hurt them!"

Paused over Enoch, Lilith grinned horribly at Cain. "Give us what we want then."

"What is it? What do you want?" Cain repeated.

The snake's voice. One word. A lifetime of misery:"You."

Desolation and despair consumed Cain. He looked at his dearly beloved mate, cowering in a corner, the Serpent holding her at bay. His eyes moved to his beautiful boy, inches from a horrendous death. Then his gaze moved to his clan, cowering behind him in fear and confusion.

"Will you leave the rest of them alone?" he asked.

"Of course," Lilith panted, staring hungrily at the scratches in her little victim's throat. "But make your decision soon. I am hungry."

She glanced at the assembled people. "Who will it be, Cain? I prefer children, but I think I can handle several meals this night."

Cain sank to the floor, despondent. "I will go with you." He didn't look up again.

Lilith dropped Enoch as if he was some dead animal. The little boy cried out in pain, and one of Cain's sisters rushed to help him. Lilith hissed menacingly at her, and she scuttled away with Enoch in tow.

The she-demon swaggered over to Cain, and held out her hand. "Come, Cain. I've missed you."

Ignoring her hand, Cain stood, eyes downcast. He turned towards the doorway, trying to block out Naya's cries. She was still pinned into the corner by the Serpent, and could not get to him.

The clan dispersed rapidly into the night as their leader and his terrifying companions left the encampment. Naya ran after him, but her sisters pulled her back. Enoch ran to her, and they clutched at each other, weeping, as they watched Cain disappear into the darkness.

"We will hunt them," said Pesah, his voice shaking and his fists clenched as he reappeared from where he had watched them go. He picked up a burning branch from the fire. "We will hunt them, and we will never rest until we have found them."

"And then?" Naya asked tearfully.

"We will destroy them." He looked darkly at Naya. "*All* of them."

Deep into the night outside of the encampment, Lilith suddenly stopped. Cain, walking desolately behind a few paces, almost ran into her.

She turned toward him, grasping his shoulders. Before he could defend himself, she had her fangs in him.

He gasped as the blood was pulled from his veins. Their constriction caused pain throughout his body, and he could feel his heartbeat, at first speeding up with the attempt to keep going, and then slowing down, dying...

He struggled against her, but she had him in a grip stronger than humanly possible. She laughed against his throat. Pulling away at last, she looked down at his nearly-dead body and smiled. He could smell his own blood, a sickly-sweet odor in the darkness. What was left within him was slowly seeping out from the wounds she had torn in his neck.

"Oh, how I have missed you," she sighed. "From now on..."

"He'll be dead," interrupted the Serpent.

"What? No!"

Even in his weakness and agony, Cain derived some pleasure at the shock in Lilith's voice. *Good. I'll be dead.* He was looking forward to it.

Lilith hissed, "He is mine. You promised."

The snake laughed hideously. "So I did. And what good does that do you?" It slithered up the two bodies, Lilith still clutching Cain. Its glare bored holes in Lilith eyes as it growled into her face. "Never forget who I am. And that you, Lilith, are here because I allow it! This man is a disappointment to me. You will kill him..."

Lilith gasped, "No, he is mine..."

"...and you will swallow his soul. He will be yours, oh yes, just not in the way you had imagined. We will keep him...available...for another time."

Cain shook his head, unbelieving. *No!* He struggled feebly. "God help me, please. Take me back..." he whispered to the stars above. Then he fainted.

A Voice came to him, and he recognized it. And he trembled.

*"Cain, you will not be lost to me. I have claimed you as Mine. Your soul will stay rooted to this life until you have completed your part in My plan."*Cain found himself floating over his own dead body. There was a pulling on his soul, but he saw no light. He was drifting slowly, but not at peace. Not like before.

He realized that he was being drawn down, down, but to where? He screeched as he was pulled into Lilith's maw. The sound echoed across the plains, once, and was no more.

PART II - JUDAS

1st Century A.D.
Bethlehem

CHAPTER 9

In the midnight quiet of a dark, silent room, a young boy lay sleeping. The moonlight cast a silvery ray of light across his peaceful little face. Dust motes danced in the light, swirling in the child's soft breath.

Something in the darkness separated itself from the rest of the shadows and moved stealthily toward the small form. The silhouette of a clawed hand blocked the light over his face; the horrible appendage flexed expectantly as its owner slowly lowered it to the boy's throat.

Lilith, panting beside the sleeping mat, knew she could take her time; the child's parents were deeply asleep in the next room. She feared no human; if they did wake up, she knew she could dispatch them soundlessly and let the rest of the inn's residents clean up the mess in the morning.

She smiled as her claws reached the child's neck, watched the pulse beat. This was her favorite part of the kill. She preferred lacerating her victims' skin rather than using her fangs. This way she could watch the crimson flow. The more her prey cried out and writhed in fright under her hands, the faster the blood would well out from the deep scratches. Finally, once she had hit a point where she couldn't wait any longer, she would finish off the kill with one quick snap of her jaws through the jugular vein. She started to dig in...

Suddenly, the midnight quiet was broken, not by the shrill scream of a dying little boy, but by a sound foreign to Lilith's ears. It seemed to be coming from outside. She allowed it to draw her attention for a mere, scant second, then turned back to concentrate again on the child.

Just a little pressure, and...

The moonlight disappeared. No, rather, it was displaced, eclipsed by a light that seemed to take over the entire night sky. The moon and the stars disappeared in a flash, except for one single, heavenly beacon.

However, this was no ordinary star. In an instant, Lilith's smile of bloodlust and triumph turned into an agonized hiss of pain. The light burned into her with an intensity that would have destroyed her had she not spun away into the shadows. As it was, her skin and hair smoked, filling the air with an acrid, terrible odor.

Either the smell, or the screech, or the glorious rays of the enormous star, woke the boy. He sat up, rubbing his eyes.

The starlight caught his attention. Fascinated by both the brilliance and the growing sounds of singing in the heavens, the boy got up. Quietly, he left his room and started downstairs. Lilith, weak and cowering in a dark corner, watched him go. She hissed angrily after him, and disappeared.

A woman emerged from a room further down the hall. A light sleeper, she had heard her son moving around, and had gotten up to see what he needed. She saw the top of his little head as he disappeared down the stairs, and called out to him:

"Judas? Where are you going?" When she didn't get an answer, she started down after him. "Judas!" she whispered loudly, "Come back here. You're going to wake everyone."

She followed him down, but stopped short as the front door of the inn came into view. Her boy was standing in the open doorway, gazing out silently into...

Daylight? How could this be? She hadn't been asleep long, she was sure of it.

But wait! The light was strange somehow.

She looked up into the sky, shocked. This wasn't sunlight! The sky wasn't daytime blue. It was still the dark of the night. The light was streaming from a huge star in the east.

The young mother approached her son and stood beside him. Outside, throngs of people filled the street. Many of Bethlehem's citizens and guests had been awakened, and had come out to see this wonder.

A hand on her shoulder startled her, and she tore her gaze from the sight. Her husband stood beside them, mesmerized by the strange light and sound. When she looked down to where Judas had been standing, he had disappeared. Grabbing her husband's arm in a panic, she almost screamed, "Simon! Where did Judas go?"

Simon blinked uncomprehendingly. "Isn't he still in bed?"

"No! He is the reason I'm up. I saw him going down the stairs. Just now he was standing right here."

They looked up and down the street.

There! Walking with a small crowd towards the gate of the town. His parents ran to catch up with him, the stones of the street barely felt in their panic. Where were they going, all these people? Why was Judas caught up with them, heedless of his mother and father running up behind him?

Why was everyone leaving town?

Now the singing reached their ears, reaching a crescendo of glorious music, tones no one on earth had ever had the privilege of hearing before. Who was singing at this time of night? The sound came from...above?

Everyone looked up at the same time. Winged, ethereal beings wafted overhead, their radiance adding to the brilliant light of the star as they floated towards the hills outside Bethlehem. The people watched the glowing assembly as it stopped over a cave cut out of a low knoll. They trailed after it, curiosity overriding any fear or trepidation they may have had.

There was a disturbance up ahead. Several shepherds were trying to make their way through the crowd to the town. "Let us through," they cried. "We must tell what we have seen!"

Simon spoke up. "Men, you can see that most of the town's inhabitants are here with you. What is more important right now than letting us go unmolested to this wonder we see before us? Tell us what it is you have seen."

The people nearby heard Simon and stopped, waiting for an answer. They all looked expectantly at the shepherds. The authority in Simon's voice made the shepherds pause. They murmured to each other, then one of their number stepped forward. His eyes were on Simon, and he pointed shakily behind him, in the direction of the singing and the light.

"These angels came to us in the fields. They told us to follow the star. We've seen...we've seen..." His voice dropped to nearly a whisper, as he closed his eyes and turned his face toward the sky. He clasped his hands before him.

"We've seen...our..." he opened his eyes and stared again at Simon, and in a firmer voice, said: "Our salvation."

Without further explanation, the shepherds backed out of the astounded assembly and disappeared back into the fields. They made their way towards the cave, which was now where the star focused its intense brilliance.

The townspeople started moving again.

Simon caught his wife's arm, and pointed. "Mira. Catch him!"

Judas' mother grabbed her son as he was about to squeeze through the milling legs of the people in front of him. He squirmed out of her hold and dashed away.

Simon and Mira called out to him, and, skirting the group ahead of them, broke into a run. Judas darted directly up the hill towards the cave, his parents following as closely as they could for all the traffic on the narrow path.

The same shepherds they had spoken to earlier were now at the mouth of the shelter. They watched as the people approached, and, in silent agreement, walked out a few paces to block the passage of the curious.

Little Judas was too quick, and dodged between them, avoiding their attempts at detaining him. Simon and Mira tried to follow, but were stopped by the bodies of the men before them.

"What is this?" Simon was indignant, and not a little irate. "Now you are stopping us again?"

Mira pleaded with the shepherds, tears in her eyes. Near panic, she looked from the men to her boy, toiling up the rocky path as fast as his little legs could take him. "Please, that is our little boy running up there!"

"There is an even smaller boy in that cave," one of the shepherds said. "It is He and His family we wish to protect." The guardian looked towards the entrance. Inside could be seen a few animals, and a couple of human figures as well. The shepherd sighed, and turned back to Mira.

Stepping aside, he spoke gently. "Please, go and get your son. We guard here a treasure beyond any earthly value, but we do not mistrust a small boy and his parents. However, we have to be careful who we let up there, and only in a controlled fashion. You will understand when you see."

He nodded to Simon, who passed between the silent sentinels with his wife. Together, they approached the mouth of the cave. The light from the star made the ground almost white with its brilliance. Simon and Mira sheltered their eyes with their hands as they squinted towards the forms within the shelter.

Once they reached the entrance, they saw a very unexpected scene. Instead of something miraculous, and glorious, and outstanding, all they saw was an ordinary man holding a small bundle of cloth, and a woman asleep on a bed of straw. The heavenly beings so evident earlier were gone, replaced by the quiet of the early hours of morning.

This treasure trove was nothing more than a stable. So what had caused such a stir among the people? All they saw were a couple of people who had obviously arrived late at night, and had had to take shelter wherever they could.

The bundle in the man's arms moved, and Mira heard a small cry. Her maternal ears knew this sound—there was a baby in that cloth. The man in the cave smiled at Mira and Simon, and gently laid the baby in a hay-filled manger. He stepped back and beckoned to them to come closer.

They walked into the entrance and looked silently at the little child. What they saw drove them to their knees in reverential awe.

The Babe looked at both of them with a gaze completely foreign to any newborn's ability. Without changing physically, it seemed he suddenly took up all time and space, filling the visitors' minds and hearts with Who He Was. A gentle glow emanated from Him......and, just as quickly, was a mere infant again, lying in the straw of the manger.

Simon and Mira blinked, looking at each other, and then back at the Baby's father. He gently smiled and nodded his head as if to say, "Yes, you did see that."

A movement to the side caught Mira's eye. Judas stood by the entrance, his finger in his mouth, staring at the infant. The boy did not move, even when Mira called softly to him. He seemed mesmerized by what he was seeing.

The light from the star changed; it suddenly cast its light full on the Baby, who did not flinch, but gazed up at it fearlessly. The light seemed to pass through a hole or fissure in the rocky roof. For just a moment, the Baby was marked by a cross-shaped beam. At the same time, the Infant looked directly at Judas.

Then the moment passed. Judas stepped slowly backwards, turned, and ran back down the hill towards the gates of Bethlehem.

CHAPTER 10

33 years later
Jerusalem

The young man stood, his back to a pillar, and watched the people around him. They were in a constant state of hurrying, either to their occupations, or to the tax collectors so they could be squeezed dry of their hard-earned wages.

Judas snorted contemptuously. *Squeezed by those Roman bastards, and thanking the tax collectors for the privilege.* Or so it seemed to him.

He crossed his arms and frowned as a widow was being harassed in the street by a couple of bored soldiers. *Probably looked at them too long. Obviously an insurgent. Well, lock her up with the rest of the rabble,* Judas thought sarcastically. *At least she'd have a roof over her head this night.*

Judas turned away. He couldn't afford to be noticed himself. Someone might recognize him, and remember his relationship with a certain Barabbas...

He gave a sharp, humorless bark of a laugh as he strolled leisurely through the marketplace. Vendors shouted, shoving their wares at him, desperate to bring in a profit before the end of the day. Judas wanted to stop and look, but he had an appointment to keep. The money in the purse at his side was heavy; lightening the load by buying himself a trinket here or there would have been both a relief and a certain amount of revenge.No. The money didn't belong to him. It belonged to all of them— the men who followed the Rabbi, leaning on his every word, letting him lead them on, making them think he was going to change the world.

Had he so far? No! Judas' hands clenched into fists when he thought of how he'd so wanted to believe this "Rabbi". Three years had come and gone, and not so much as a suggestion of raising an army. Not even a rusty sword bought in defense of the people of Israel. *When was he going to act?*

He'd certainly had the people of Jerusalem all for him a few days ago, when he'd entered the gates on a donkey. Oh, he knew the Scriptures, and certainly had done the right thing to get noticed. Then, just when the people were getting to riot stage, he'd disappeared.

And the Roman soldiers came with their swords and menace, and everyone ducked their heads to the grindstone once again. *Well*, Judas thought, his pace quickening, *there is one other who will do what the Rabbi will not.*

That was the man Judas was meeting.

At the end of the rows of market stalls, Judas caught the eye of a certain beggar. He was sitting against the wall at the edge of the marketplace, looking more like a bundle of rags and discarded belongings than a man.

The beggar nodded surreptitiously, then called out to Judas, pleading with outstretched arms. Judas walked past him, and dropped a token into his cupped hands. He walked past, and stopped.

Peering around, Judas pretended he was looking for something on the ground. Meanwhile, the old beggar examined Judas' gift carefully, nodded approval, and tapped the wall behind him with his walking stick.

Immediately, two large and well-scarred men appeared out of nowhere. They carried no weapons, but Judas was certain that they could do just as well in a fight without them.

They glanced at the beggar. He looked pointedly at Judas, who was still perusing the ground for whatever object he had "lost".

The two men came alongside Judas. One whispered a word, and Judas fell in step between them, all three looking furtively around the marketplace and up at the tops of the walls, making sure no one had given them undue attention. Then the trio disappeared into a potter's tent, and from there to an inner room behind it.

It took a moment for Judas' eyes to adjust to the candlelit darkness. The smoky interior seemed to bristle with muscle-bound, hostile individuals. They all glared at him, and Judas stopped in his tracks. Just as he was about to turn on his heel and run, his arms were gripped hard by his escorts, and he was propelled forward. His eyes grew wide with fright, and his heart pounded as he was drawn nearer to the band of outlaws.

The group encircled its hapless visitor, keeping wary eyes on him. Judas could see some of them flexing their muscles and slowly curling their hands into fists. He tried hard to conceal his terror, suppressing his trembling and not looking at any of them directly.

The tension was broken by loud laughter from somewhere behind the group. Several of the outlaws were pushed aside as a burly man barged his way through the ring. Judas relaxed, although not entirely, as he recognized the newcomer.

It was Barabbas.

He looked Judas up and down with disdain. A deep, slow chuckle emanated from his bristly beard, but the humor did not reach his eyes. "Judas Iscariot. Well, well. Didn't think I'd live to see the day." Judas gave Barabbas a sickly smile, then turned away from his penetrating glare. The insurgent continued, "What brings you back to our illustrious circle?" He waved his arm to include the brigands surrounding his guest. Some of them grunted humorlessly; two spit, nearly hitting Judas' feet. All kept their steely gaze on him.

Their chief flicked his gaze at Judas' captors, who released him immediately. Judas rubbed his arms where they had clutched him. "Things...didn't work out. This man Jesus was not who I thought he'd be. I...made a mistake."

"And now you're coming back, full of remorse, and you think that you can just walk back in here and we'd welcome you with open arms."

The look on Judas' face told it all: yes, he'd surmised that.

Barabbas shook his head slowly, his teeth showing through his beard in a mocking smile. "You innocent. How do we know you're not a spy? Even now, half of my men are watching for any detritus you might have dragged here with you."

"I was careful. I did everything exactly as I was told. You know me, Barabbas. I wouldn't betray my own."

"Still, we'd be stupid to allow you in without some sort of guarantee of your loyalty. We let you go...once. That part was easy. To get back in, you'll have to prove yourself."

Judas gulped nervously. Thoughts of murder and pillage flashed through his mind. He had never imagined himself at the action end of this gang's activity. He'd always been a planner. To get his hands bloodied, even to prove himself worthy of membership, had not been something he'd considered. Perhaps he'd been too hasty in coming back here. Now, however, it was impossible to back out.

He tried to look calm and in control, but his palms were sweating. Meeting Barabbas' gaze, he asked, "How do I do that?"

The robber-chief held out a giant, calloused paw, pointing towards the coin purse Judas had hidden within the folds of his garments.

Eyes wide, Judas clutched at the bag. The faces of the brothers—his friends—flashed through his mind. "I...I can't give this away. This money was entrusted to me. It...it isn't mine. It belongs to..."

"To the group of sheep you no longer wish to associate yourself with. Am I right? Or am I mistaken?"

Judas couldn't answer him. After all, these "sheep" had befriended him, had become family to him. They had done nothing to deserve his departure from them. He had never felt as much a sense of belonging as when he had followed Jesus.

What was he doing here, and now that he had reconsidered, how was he going to get away? He couldn't exactly say, "I've changed my mind, good day to you," and just walk out of the place. They'd kill him before he had taken one step towards the doorway.

His dilemma was solved for him when a crash and much shouting erupted at the front of the tent. Suddenly the dark place was flooded with light, as the tent walls were pulled down and soldiers rushed in, brandishing their weapons. Knives flashed from the folds of bandit clothing as the insurgents set upon the invaders with a howl of rebellious rage.

In the melee, Judas managed to dodge and duck his way to freedom with little injury. He pushed his way into the crowd in the marketplace, going against the tide of curious onlookers intent on watching this impromptu entertainment. Sidling quickly between the throng and the wall of the city, he managed to finally find a niche where he could hide.

Heart pounding, Judas sat on the steps in the small alcove, drawing his knees up to his chest and hugging his legs to his body. He ducked his head down and tried to look as small as possible as he watched for signs of anybody who might be pursuing him.

The milling crowd suddenly parted, and Roman soldiers marched through their midst. Barabbas was among the dozen or so insurgents who were being dragged, carried, or escorted at spear point toward the prison grounds. The rest of the rebels had scattered, to await another day and another chance at freedom.

Judas smiled grimly to himself. *That was close. Time to get back to the brethren*, he smiled with genuine warmth at the thought, *and just keep out of trouble.*

They were all probably hungry by now, and the markets were about to close. Since he carried the group's treasury, it was up to him to buy some food, and he knew the best market to go to.

He got up, brushed off his clothes, and felt for the coin purse.

His heart froze within him.

It was gone!

CHAPTER 11

Now there was no pretense, no acting as if he'd lost something. He was truly in trouble. Frantically, he retraced his steps back to where the beggar had been, up against the wall of the city. Maybe he would be able to...

No!

The beggar was one of the brigands, although he had probably been able to escape arrest. The poor were always overlooked, simply because they were always there. The man had probably just folded up his mat and walked away.

Judas looked anyway. Yes, he was gone. No one in the milling crowd seemed to notice that the potter's booth had also vanished, even to the tent poles and shards of broken clay that were usually around such a place. The populace of Jerusalem didn't dare notice; they knew that too many questions led to a place on the crucifixion scaffold. Judas shuddered at the thought.

He'd seen those frames stretched across the outside of the city walls. More than once, the bodies of those who thought they could oppose Rome had filled them to capacity. It was a sight he did not want to see again. The problem was that not enough Jews banded together to rise up and overpower the occupying forces. They were cowed by the Romans and lulled by the leaders, who kept telling them to "be patient".

Walking slowly, looking carefully along the street in what he knew was a vain effort, Judas felt the old frustration return. "'Be patient'." If only people would stop being such timid mice, complaining behind closed doors, and actually organize something. Yes, but who would lead them? Not insurgents like Barabbas—too violent. He scared people, got arrested time and time again, and was more interested in what he could thieve off others rather than bringing a united front to the rebellion.

Judas knew that Jesus could lead them all. He could fix all of their ills: physical, spiritual, but most of all, political. *If only he would.*

His thoughts were suddenly cut off by the sound of shouting. Looking up, he realized that he was now right outside of the walls of the Temple. The shouting was coming from somewhere inside the courtyard.

What could be going on in there? Judas rushed toward the sound, passing others heading in the same direction. It seemed an odd place for a riot. That area was reserved for the vendors who sold animals for sacrifice. True, not the area's original intent, but once the merchants got in and struck a deal with the temple officials, no one stood in the way.

Maybe someone was robbed, although that seemed unlikely. So many Temple guards, all armed to the teeth. No one could get away with thieving within those walls. Herod's puppets wouldn't dare let a single errant shekel roll out of the gates without chasing it down. Heaven forbid that Rome should lose even that little.

Judas pushed his way through the wall of curiosity-seekers into the temple courtyard. As he got closer to the owner of that angry voice, he suddenly stopped. Behind him, an old man was nearly trampled as he fell against Judas' back. Judas caught him, righted him, and ran off as best he could through the throng, heedless of the man's cries of gratitude.

Judas had neither time nor ears for anything or anyone. He plunged forward, taking his chances in angering the larger, taller men in his way. He knew that voice. Hadn't he spent three years listening to its owner? Counseling, teaching, healing, laughing as he held the children who loved him so.

Judas was finally close enough to see why everyone was in such a stir. He peeped over a shoulder in front of him, confirming what he had already surmised, and quickly ducked into a merchant stall to await the outcome. Judas knew that it was only a matter of time before the guards would be upon Jesus, to either throw him out or arrest him.

Peeking out from his vantage point, he could see that the Rabbi was holding a whip of some sort. His face was flushed with anger. Looking around at the vendors, he suddenly lashed out with the whip. Judas flinched as he imagined some poor unlucky soul being stung by its tail, but the cord wrapped around the leg of a moneychanger's table, sending it crashing to the ground.

Judas was surprised, and more than pleased. This was unbelievable! His Rabbi was inciting a riot! He looked around the assembly, waiting to see who would take the next step. It would be easy enough to flank the guards, who stood watching the spectacle. After all, they seemed as stunned as everyone else in the courtyard; the only ones moving were the merchants, who were scrambling to collect and protect their wares and profits.

That's odd, Judas suddenly thought, looking around. Where was the merchant for the booth he himself was hiding in? Judas suddenly realized that he was alone in the tent. He stepped further into its recesses, ready to run at a moment's notice.

The booth seemed deserted. No doubt the owner was off being entertained by the one-man riot. He'd be back soon, for Jesus was making his way around to all of the tents, and would soon be at this one.

Judas was about to slip out of the booth's cool interior, on his way to another viewpoint, when he spied a moneybag on a table near the back.

An idea hit him: take the bag, and the problem of the group's loss would be solved.

Looking out through the booth entrance, Judas glanced at the crowd to see if anyone had noticed him. Satisfied that they were still watching the angry man decimating the stalls, he slipped the coin purse into his clothing and walked out into the daylight. Soon he had blended in with the rest of the onlookers.

Not too far from the main entrance, he found the rest of the Brethren. They were huddled close together, muttering worriedly amongst themselves.

James was the first to catch sight of Judas, and hurried to him as fast as the crowd would allow. "Where have you been?"

"Never mind," retorted Judas, his eyes on the Teacher. "What is he up to? Is he trying to provoke everyone to riot against the Romans? About time." Judas grabbed James' shoulders. He stared excitedly into the startled man's eyes. "Are we to overpower the guards? Where's my dagger? What part are we playing in this revolt? Where are the others who are to back us up? Why are we just standing here?"

James finally was able to get in a word. "Judas, calm down. It's not like that. No one is trying to incite a riot."

Judas' face fell. All this excitement for nothing...

James sighed. "You know that the Master isn't trying to take over Jerusalem. He's told us that time and time again. He wants the people to turn to God and be free in their hearts, no matter who their earthly ruler is."

Judas flung his arm angrily towards where Jesus, now winded and apparently through with his tirade, was tossing aside the whip. Tables were toppled, money and goods strewn all around him. "Then what was this...*show*...all about?"

Peter had walked over and joined the two men. He explained, "We were simply going towards the Temple to pray, and Jesus suddenly stopped walking. We could see him staring at the merchant booths, and suddenly he got this look in his eye. Strange—he'd seen all of this before, but this time he seemed to be insulted by them.

"He told us to stay here and wait for him, and that's when he rushed out and started overturning tables. Then he started shouting something about this being 'a house of prayer, not a nest of thieves'."

Judas rubbed his eyes and shook his head. *All this noise for that? Was the Rabbi finally losing his hold on reality? What was his complaint with a system that had been in place even before any of them had been born?*

The buzz of the crowd rose again, as a handful of Roman soldiers marched into the temple courtyard, bristling with weapons. People suddenly found something else to do, and very soon there was quiet and order again. No one could be found in the area who wasn't supposed to be there.

And that included Jesus…

He had somehow vanished!

The disciples were both startled and perplexed. Where had he gone? As one, they started out into the light of the courtyard, spreading out to search for their leader. A voice from behind them made them stop before they had taken too many steps.

"I am right here with you." It was Jesus, right there in their midst.

Judas shook his head in amazement. If only he could get around as quickly and noiselessly as that…

"Judas."

The voice, so angry and loud only a few minutes ago, now seemed very quiet, seemingly for Judas' ears only.

"Yes, Rabbi?"

"The bag." Jesus was holding out his hand, palm up. Judas couldn't look him in the face; he turned away, gripping his cloak about him. *How could he have known? When did he see me?*

"What bag?" he asked the ground at his feet.

"The one you took from the merchant's stall."

Judas started, and turned startled eyes to his Master. "I...I don't know what you mean. All I have is our money. Our coin purse."

Jesus shook his head slowly. His eyes held no accusation, no recrimination. Just love, and...something else...

Without breaking the gaze between them, Judas pulled the pouch out from his cloak, and, as if in a trance, handed it over to Jesus. The Rabbi turned and walked back into the courtyard, the Brethren close behind. Judas walked beside him, not because he wanted to, but because he didn't want to meet the angry gazes and hear the whispered remarks of the other disciples. He was not looking forward to meeting up with the rightful owner of that money.

Jesus knew exactly where he was going. How he knew, Judas could not fathom. After all, he knew that Jesus had had his back to him when he had taken the bag.

The merchant looked up from his counting table; then, when he saw who had come in, got up and backed away quickly, eyes wide.

"Wh-what do you want here? I'm packing up as fast as I can. Just trying to work out how much I owe the temple officials. I..."

"Don't worry," Jesus assured him. "We're here because one of our number took a bag of coins from your stall."

"What?" The merchant looked from face to face, sudden righteous anger building up within him.

Jesus looked at Judas, who swallowed hard and stepped forward. His face flushed, he stammered out a response. "I'm s...sorry. I shouldn't have done what I did. Here is your money pouch."

Jesus handed the man his coins. The vendor grabbed it away, his eyes flashing. "Oh, you will be," he growled at Judas, "when I send the temple guards after you. You..."

Jesus laid a hand on the enraged man's arm. "Please forgive him. I will make sure this doesn't happen again."

The anger seemed to lift immediately from the merchant. He looked a little confused, seeming to argue with himself under his breath. Turning away from the group, he stood for a moment, quietly considering.

Then he turned back. All animosity was gone. He stepped up to Judas and said firmly, "I can forgive you this once, but I never want to see you again."

Judas ducked his head in silent reply, and quickly exited the tent before the others. Squinting in the sunlight, he suddenly saw, with sinking heart, two very familiar faces. Across the courtyard from him were a couple of Barabbas' men. Apparently they had been some of the lucky few who had escaped being arrested.

They'd seen him too. One of the men gave him a wide, humorless smile, and held up an object.

The Brethren's money purse!

The other flashed a sword from under his cloak. They pulled themselves off the wall they'd been casually slouching against, and started walking toward him. The look of menace in their eyes told Judas that they were not about to pay a social call.

He made a mad dash toward the entryway, hoping he could outrun them and find a place to hide until they were far away. Judas knew, with a thief's heart and mind, that this would be an entirely unsafe area to operate out of for quite some time. The bandits would not spend any more time here than they had to.

He plunged through the milling populace, making twists and turns through city streets, until he came to a row of large, comfortable-looking homes. A gate to one of them hung open, as if inviting him in. Judas took no thought of caution as he bolted through it, and then through a narrow door into an inner courtyard.

No one seemed to stir from within the house as Judas stood just inside the terraced courtyard, panting from exertion. He ducked behind a large water cistern to wait out the day, until he felt it would be safe to get up and find his way back to the brothers.

CHAPTER 12

Afternoon turned to early evening. Judas grew bored and restless, waiting for full darkness so that he could escape undetected. He'd long ago finished perusing the little garden from behind the cistern. Nothing fantastic or even remotely interesting was planted within these walls.

The fading twilight had very little to occupy itself within this place. Most of the ground was floored with large, flat slabs of stone. The few plants that ringed its edges were straggly, and were being choked out by weeds and undergrowth. The wall of the house that was attached to this small plot of...nothing...was unadorned, save for a simple door that seemed to turn in on itself. In the right light, it could almost seem as if the portal was trying to hide from the world it looked out on.

The only item of interest was the tall water vessel Judas was hiding behind. It was made of alabaster, which was not uncommon in itself. Its interest lay in the milky color of the stone. It seemed almost translucent when viewed from the right angle. Judas whiled away the time by studying the cistern's surface fissures and the way the remaining light seemed to make it come alive. As night came on, he grew drowsy, having spent all of his energy on the day's adventures with no food to replenish it.

As he gazed drowsily at the alabaster, his mind wandered back to another day, and other water cisterns made of stone.

It had been a glorious day. The season had not yet turned to the brilliant fire of summer; it was still pleasant enough for leisurely daytime activities. He well remembered the morning of his distant cousin's wedding. The sun rose through a fine mist, which burned off in time for the celebration.

It was a good match. The bride was beautiful, the groom radiant, the parents more than content in their decision. Everyone in the wedding party seemed to like each other. All were happy with the ceremony, and even happier when it was over. Because that was when the feast started.

Ah, the food. The wine. So much! The only thing missing, in Judas' mind, was the love of his life.

Jayla.

Beautiful, exotic Jayla. Judas grew sad with the memory.

She had appeared as if by magic, riding into his hometown, and into his heart, such a short time ago. Big, dark eyes framed by long, soft lashes, a laugh that could charm flowers into blooming, and a heart that held the world in it.

Quite simply, she was lovely. And she loved.

They had met in the marketplace. Jayla had been plaiting reeds, the gold threads in her headdress brilliant in the sun as she bent her head to her task.

Judas had been helping his mother find what she needed for the week. She was the first to spy the girl's work; Jayla's baskets lay about her in a seemingly planned chaos.

"Judas," and her claw of a hand pulled her son's arm, "I want to see these."

He remembered rolling his eyes and guiding her over to where Jayla was plying her trade. What did his mother need with yet more things? His father had died years ago, and she was just a breath away from Sheol, yet she bought new delights as feverishly as a newlywed.

In an instant, all of his negative feelings vanished, as Jayla looked up at them.

At him.

The world, for Judas, started turning at that moment.

He didn't remember what they said, or what his mother purchased, or what went on the rest of the day. He did, however, remember where the basket booth was, and sought her out the next afternoon. And the next.

Months went on like this. He knew he was in love, and she seemed to feel the same way. It was a thing never discussed, their feelings for each other. Judas always meant to say something to her, but it never seemed the right time. Besides, her father or brothers were always nearby, glowering at him from under dark, threatening eyebrows.

Then, just days ago, when he went to see her, his world abruptly ended.

They were gone.

He looked, he asked, he thought over everything they had said the day before. Had she mentioned that they were leaving? No, he would have remembered.

The heart of a nomad—no matter how it became fond of another, it would always love the road more. She was gone—off to another town, another marketplace. The dust of yet another journey would stain that lovely face an even darker brown, and another heart would break when she left him too.

So here he was at his cousin's wedding, with his elderly mother of all people. All around him, young people his age were conversing and laughing with each other, starting the germination of relationships to come, for good or ill, and here he sat, making sure his mother wiped the food from her chin...

He took another drink of wine, and signaled to a nearby servant for a refill. The young man came to him, and poured a ruby-red nectar from an ewer. He leaned over to Judas and whispered, "Best get your fill now, for we are almost out of wine."

Judas couldn't believe it.

No more wine? Who planned this wedding feast? That man should be flogged! The guests would not stay if the wine ran out, and the family would be disgraced.

"Thank you for telling me," he managed to get out. The servant nodded once, and went back to his place against the wall.

Judas wondered if anyone else knew. No one seemed to be acting any differently than they had an hour before. Maybe he was the only one, besides the wine boy, who knew. Why would the servant tell him, of all people?

He turned to ask him, but the man had disappeared.

"What were you talking about?" asked Judas' mother, whose hearing was not what it used to be.

Judas leaned over to her. "He said they are almost out of wine," he whispered loudly into her ear.

"Would we what? Want to dine? I thought we did." She looked confused for a moment. "Didn't we?"

Judas' heart sank. His poor mother seemed to forget more and more every day.

"No, Mother." Judas raised his voice a little louder, hoping to hit the right level so that she could hear him, but no one else. "He said there's no more wine."

"Oh! Is that right?" She smiled at her son, then a look of shock suddenly replaced her contented demeanor. "What?" she exclaimed loudly. "No wine! That's terrible!"

Her voice seemed to echo around the room. Judas glanced wildly at those seated nearby, but to his relief, apparently no one had heard her over the general noise of the hundreds of wedding guests.

"Please, Mother, not so loud. I'll see what I can do."

Mira sat still, the contented smile on her face once more, staring into space.

Well, there's one person who doesn't need any more wine, thought Judas. He sighed and started to stand up.

A cool, gentle hand on his arm stopped him. He looked at its owner, startled that a woman would touch him, and a stranger at that.

His heart melted within him. The woman was, quite simply, beautiful. She was much older than her beauty, but her loveliness seemed to be an eternal gift. It was the radiance of heaven's own love. Judas didn't know how he knew this. He just knew.

Before he could do or say anything, the woman smiled gently at him and said, "I heard about the wine running out. I believe I can help."

"Who are you?" Judas blurted out. Then, apologetically, "I mean, how can you be...that is to say, are you related to the bride or groom? I was going to go talk to them..."

"But you don't really know them, do you?"

Judas was flabbergasted. *How did she know?*

She noted the astonished look on his face, and patted his arm maternally. "Your position in the room. Close family is further up, closer to the wedding party. Like me, you are more distantly related. Leave it to me. I know...someone...who can take care of the wine problem."

Judas looked into her eyes. She looked confident enough, but somehow doubtful at the same time. It was as if she knew her plan would work with no problem, as long as she had cooperation from that "someone".

He shook his head. *Women!*

"I was going to go and talk discreetly to the groom's father, since my father was friends with him..." he started.

"No, please," she almost pleaded, "let me take care of this. It's important."

She rose and walked away. Judas shrugged, and watched her wend her way through the people ranged around the banquet hall. She stopped at the side of a young man, who was seated with several friends, and laid a hand on his shoulder.

At once, the man turned his full, loving attention on her. They whispered to each other, and Judas could see them become more and more animated as the conversation went on. It looked as if she was trying to convince him of something.

The man finally grasped the woman's hands, smiled gently at her, and nodded his consent. She beamed at him, and, kissing him on the forehead, returned to her seat beside Judas and Mira.

She leaned over to Judas and whispered, "That's my son. Watch what happens." She sat back, smiling, her attention on the events unfolding on the other side of the room.

Her son called over one of the servants and spoke to him. The young man bowed and hurried away. Within a few minutes, an older man came hurrying, with the servant beside him. He wore the garb of one in higher authority, and he smiled and bobbed his head at the group of young men at the table.

After a moment's conversation, his look changed abruptly to one of alarm. He whispered something to the servant standing at his side, who nodded miserably.

"The wine steward," came a voice at Judas' ear. He nodded absentmindedly, his attention on what was being enacted at that table.

The steward turned to march off, fire in his eyes. Judas smiled humorlessly; obviously someone below this man had not followed through with his assigned task. That one would be the first person in a series of beatings, no doubt.

The young man, this woman's son, caught the steward's arm as he prepared to storm off. He cast his glance one time towards his mother, who nodded encouragement.

His eyes then traveled to Judas', and the two locked gazes on each other. At that precise moment, something changed in Judas. He didn't know why or how, but he knew that his life would be different from now until forever—and he wasn't ready for that. He didn't know if he'd ever be ready.

Those eyes. Such gentleness, but such authority! In them were wisdom and innocence, love and power, here and now; yesterday, today, and tomorrow. They beckoned him with gladness, with promise, with hope.

And, somehow, with a certain degree of sadness.

A push at his arm. Surprised, Judas looked to his side.

To his own mother. She had followed his gaze, and somehow, through her mental fog, a light of clarity had shown. "Go."

Judas' eyes widened in astonishment. "Go? Go where? I'm not going anywhere. You...you can't live alone. Who would care for you?" The words he blurted confused him. *No one had mentioned leaving hearth and home. What am I thinking?*

"I'll be fine," Mira assured him. "He wants you to follow him, to learn from him. The Lord God will look after me."

"Oh?" Judas asked sarcastically. "Will He come to your house, and cook and clean for you? Will He take you to the market and wait endless hours for you to decide what useless dross you're going to buy? Is He going to..."

Mira slapped her son's face. Not hard; just enough to stop the rising anger that they both knew was difficult to master once it was unleashed. She shook a finger in his face.

"Careful, my son. The events that will take place in this room today will carry much further than our miserable little lives."

Such words! Judas could only gape at his mother, who just as suddenly went back to staring mutely at the son of the woman at Judas' other side.

This one once again touched his arm. He looked over at her. She gave him that same beatific smile and said, "Don't worry about your mother. I will make sure she is taken care of. You go to my son. His name is Jesus."

Judas looked back and forth at the two women as if both had lost their minds. Finally he came to a decision. "I'll go over there and spend the rest of the day with them. Then I am going *home,* with my *mother*!"

He rose and stalked off. *Why were they trying to get rid of me all of a sudden?* Certainly Jesus' mother must be close to the same age as his own mother? How could two old women possibly fend for each other? It didn't make any sense.

Well, they could make all the silly plans they wished. He knew where he'd be laying his head tonight—in his own bed, thank you.

As he approached Jesus and his friends, Judas spotted much activity through the open doorway into the kitchen. Forgetting the enigmatic young man and his followers for a moment, Judas leaned on the doorpost to watch what was going on.

For some odd reason, the wine steward was supervising a large group of servants who were...filling cisterns with water?? Every now and then, he would look back at Jesus and shake his head, a bemused expression on his face.

Now why, in the midst of this urgent need for more wine, were they all scurrying around doing such an unnecessary thing? No one was going to accept water in place of their favorite drink. Surely the head steward must be drunk, or an idiot.

Judas watched as the portly man came thundering out of the kitchen, dodging as he almost ran into him. A few servants followed him out, running to keep pace. Confusion and frustration were plain on his face. Apparently this was not his idea; however, he had no choice but to carry it out.

The steward strode briskly over to Jesus, and whispered something to him. Jesus answered, and the steward gave one of his underlings an order.

The servant hurried back to the kitchen, as confused as the wine steward. Judas watched the servant grab a cup and fill it with water from the cisterns. He sniffed it, shrugged, and took a sip. He shook his head and rushed back to the steward. Giving the cup to him, he backed away, staring at Jesus as if he was a madman.

The steward took a look at the contents of the cup.

Judas happened to glance at Jesus, and was alarmed at what he saw. Jesus' eyes were closed, and he had broken out in a cold sweat. His skin had paled, and he gripped the table with white-knuckled hands.This lasted for mere moments. Indeed, it seemed to Judas that he had imagined what he had seen.

A stifled cry of surprise made Judas look back at the steward.

The man had taken a sip from the cup, and a look of wonderment came over him. He stared at Jesus in awe, unable to move. Jesus touched the man's arm, and gestured for him to go make the wine available. The steward gathered his wits and sped off to the kitchen, barking orders to get the wine flasks filled again. There was still much celebrating to be done.

Judas stayed at his post in the doorway, thinking everyone had finally lost their minds.

A serving girl went by with several cups of the water, and Judas signaled for one of them. She smiled sweetly and offered one up to him. He took it and looked into its depths, much as the steward had done. He sniffed it, and jerked his head back in surprise.

Wine!

But he had seen them fill those cisterns from the water supply outside. Maybe there was just a perfume added that made the water smell like this...

His first sip convinced him otherwise. This was the best wine he had ever tasted...and he had had plenty of occasions to taste a lot of wine. Never had he experienced such a perfect harmony of flavors.

He had to know. *How?*

Judas walked over to where Jesus was once again engaged in a lively conversation with the group at his table. Not wanting to interrupt, he stopped a ways off, and bided his time by studying this strange man.

As Judas tried to think of some way of approaching him, Jesus suddenly turned and focused those powerful eyes and that gentle smile on him again.

"Welcome, Judas. Won't you join us?"

CHAPTER 13

Untold time passed as Judas lay stretched out behind the cistern. He passed in and out of sleep, lulled by the memories of his time in Jesus' company. The past three years had been the best ones of his life, even with the discomfort of the poverty Jesus chose to live in.

When he finally came fully awake, night had taken full hold of the world. Stars shone bright in the moonless sky above him, and night insects buzzed their songs in the evening air. He closed his eyes again, trying to draw back the comforting dreams he had just left. As his mind spiraled up into consciousness, he noticed that his hand was very cold, which caused him some vague alarm. Then he realized that he was still touching the stone water vessel.

Of course! he thought, and took his hand from its surface. He put his fingers into his armpit, trying to get them warmed up again. Then he started to drift off once more, deciding that another hour's sleep would be very welcome.

He was just dropping off into full slumber when he became gradually aware of another sensation. Something very cold was touching his shoulder. The realization woke him with a jolt; his first thought was that Barabbas' minions had found him and were about to lay cold steel to his throat.

With a cry, he sat up, ready to defend himself. He was not at all prepared for the vision that greeted his eyes.

The cistern was gone. In its place stood an extraordinarily beautiful woman. She was clothed in milky-white, almost translucent raiment, with a shimmering black headdress. The scarf was arranged so that it fell over her shoulders, but it did not hide her lovely face.

Such alluring eyes, and such ruby-red lips! Her skin was almost as pale as her garment, the overall effect being that she looked as if she was glowing in the dark.

It seemed as if she smiled down on him, but Judas couldn't be certain. What light there was played tricks on his eyes; one moment she seemed to be an ordinary young lady, perhaps the inhabitant of this house, and the next she seemed...odd somehow. Judas couldn't put a finger on it...

Her voice made him put away any misgivings he might have had. It fell from her lips in a rich, mellifluous tone, like the ringing of many bells in harmony with time and nature.

"And who are you, to be in my garden at this time of night?" There was no threat or fear in her tone, merely curiosity.

She sat down next to him, right on the soil of the garden. Her perfume permeated his senses; it was of a type he had never known. Somewhat like flowers, but then again like incense, and in the next moment like an aromatic wood. It both pleased and confused him.

He forced himself to concentrate on her question. "Um..."

Why was it so difficult to get his thoughts in order? He must be more tired than he thought.

"'Um.' This is all you can say? I go outside to walk in my garden and find a strange man sleeping behind my water jar, and all I have as an answer is 'um'?" Her face showed no anger. Indeed, she seemed somehow amused. Her voice had a hint of teasing in it.

"No, I mean..." Judas sighed and tried again. "What I mean is, I was in the street outside, and I have nowhere to stay," this was probably true; the Brothers would have his head if he went back to them now, "and this garden looked deserted. So I thought I might just stay for the night..."

She stopped him with a finger on his lips. With hooded eyes, she drew nearer. The headdress suddenly seemed to undulate in the deepening twilight; Judas sucked in his breath and moved back at what he thought he had seen.

The woman looked surprised. She peered at him questioningly. "Why are you so frightened?"

Judas gathered himself together. "Nothing...just a trick of the light. Sorry."

Nonetheless, he was beginning to feel nervous in the company of this stranger. Her headdress, he could see now, was nothing more than it should be. However, something was just not right with her...

She seemed to sense his nervousness, and started to smile. Then, just as those sensuous lips parted to reveal her teeth, she covered the lower part of her face with the black veil. Touching his hand, she stared at him. "I know why you're here...Judas."

He started in surprise and quickly jumped to his feet, ready to run or fight. Her laughter stopped him in mid-action; he looked down at her, sitting comfortably on the ground. "Do not think me strange, Judas. You are known to me. I have seen you with your mother, and with the one you call 'Rabbi'."

She looked serious now. "I saw his actions in the Temple precincts today. That was very dangerous."

Judas sat back down at her side, puzzled but no longer afraid. She was merely a woman and no more. She'd been in the crowd today. What had he been thinking? He laughed a little self-consciously.

"What is so amusing?" the woman asked, a bit of amusement in her own voice.

"I...well, I just haven't been myself since I woke up. Just...sorry, it seemed odd that you know who I am, and I..."

"Know nothing of me, yes?"

Judas blinked, and looked over at her. *No, not exactly that, but then again...*

He found himself caught in her gaze. She drew him in somehow, but it certainly wasn't a bad feeling...

"Yes...I think..." In truth, Judas didn't know what to think, or how, or truly anything anymore. He only knew those dark, luminous eyes, like the moon in shadow, but not quite like that at all...

"Your Rabbi. His actions will bring only more ill will towards him. I am concerned, as are all the people who live here. Actions like that will cause the Romans to send in more troops, and we don't need to feed and lodge more bodies in this city than we already have. Don't you agree, Judas?"

"I..."

Just then, a servant entered the garden from the street. He stood far away from the woman, waiting until she acknowledged his presence. "Yes, Adon?" She looked sideways at him.

Her glance caused Adon to step back. He flinched as if he feared his mistress.

She held out a hand to the young boy. "Come, Adon. What would you tell me?" Her voice was warm and gentle; Judas couldn't imagine how anyone could fear her.

Perhaps his imagination; he really did need to find a comfortable, quiet place to get some decent sleep. He had almost forgotten the feel of a sleeping mat under his tired body.

It was deep night now—no more twilight. They had been conversing in complete darkness for who knew how long. He peered over at Adon, barely visible in the short distance to the gate.

The boy stepped out of the garden and returned quickly with a torch that had been put up outside the wall. The light was almost blinding; Judas put a hand in front of his face, peering out between his fingers.

Adon came closer and spoke to his mistress. "Lady Lilith, I have done as you wished. Your water jar is filled."

The boy's voice trembled. The light on his face revealed drops of sweat on his brow. He glanced once at Judas, who was shocked at the sheer terror in the younger man's eyes.

Adon unconsciously put a hand to his swathed throat as his gaze went back to Lilith. She gave him a warning look, and then said, "Very good. You may retire for the night. But," and here she uncovered her face in Adon's direction, "be ready to come to me if I should need you."

Adon whimpered and, turning, ran off into the dark, dropping the torch on the stones as he fled.

Lilith laughed quietly. "Such a good boy, but so afraid of the night. I cannot understand why."

She turned back to Judas, the scarf across her face once more. "Are you afraid of the dark, Judas?" She leaned close to him.

"N...no, I've never had reason to be." He was surprised to find himself trembling.

Lilith noticed. "Oh, you must be cold. It is still early in the year. I don't notice it that much somehow. Come inside. I imagine you are hungry."

Judas seemed to remember hunger. Come to think of it, he hadn't eaten since hours before his ill-fated meeting with Barabbas.

Lilith rose to her feet. She took his hand and led him towards the lone door in the wall of the house. He followed docilely.

Then he heard her laugh to herself: "I know I certainly am thirsty."

Odd. Her head covering once again seemed to shimmer and move. In the dim light of the stars and the faint light cast by the discarded torch, Judas imagined it somehow winding itself tighter around Lilith's neck. She caught at it casually and pulled it loose. It stayed that way, but Judas sensed a strange frustration in her. Cautiously now, he followed her, but at a distance. As he passed by the sputtering torch, he picked it up, carrying it at arm's length ahead of him.

"Do we really need that, Judas? We were doing just fine without it."

"Yes, but that was before…"

"Before what?" Her eyes teased him.

"Umm…before Adon brought it in." Yes, that sounded right. "Now I'd like to have the light with me." He couldn't tell her his real thoughts: that this very well could be a trap, and that there was trouble waiting in the recesses of that house. He had a sudden realization: not the least of that trouble might be Lilith herself.

Lilith sighed. "Oh, very well. If you must."

She disappeared into the building. Judas followed, every sense pricked, sweeping the torch around as he walked inside. Shadows ran from the light, but no brigands jumped from corners.

It couldn't be helped, this distrust of strange surroundings. He was well aware of the various ways the unlawful could take a man unawares. His life was forfeit as long as Barabbas' men were at large. It would be foolhardy to assume that they would believe that he had no part in the raid that day, and there were those in the lower echelons of Jerusalem who would drag him before the remnants of that crew for a shekel.

That delicious laugh of Lilith's again, just beyond the reach of the torchlight. "They are not here. We are quite alone."

"What?" *How did she know?* Unless she knew that they were indeed here, and was lying...

"Barabbas' men. I saw you being pursued by them. I know that band, believe me. We are somewhat of the same mind, and have crossed paths many times. Now come, sit beside me."

She had dropped onto some cushions in a far corner of the room. Judas took another glance around before joining her. The room was small and almost bare of furnishings. There was one other door besides the one to the garden, and was in the opposite wall. Both seemed firmly closed. The only items large enough to hide behind were a table and a few chairs, and there was no one lurking there.

Judas relaxed a little, and took a seat on a cushion to Lilith's right, keeping a cautious distance between them. He kept the torch in his hand, however; no sense letting down his guard completely. He hadn't survived his adult years and occasional misadventures without learning a few important survival skills. Even now, he could feel his arms flexing, readying themselves for anything. If someone burst in, he was ready to fight. No one could overpower Judas Iscariot in fair—or unfair—combat.

Lilith watched him, a smile in her eyes. Suddenly she exclaimed, "Oh, I did promise you something to eat. Wait here. I will be back shortly." In one fluid movement, she was on her feet and through the inner door. Her white form moved mist-like into the darkness where the fire's light did not reach.

While she was gone, Judas decided that it would be a good idea to put the torch up so that the light spread through the room further. He found a wall sconce above his head, and affixed the firebrand into it.

Within minutes, Lilith was back, carrying a loaf of bread and a pomegranate on a small silver plate. She also held two matching silver cups and a jug filled with a dark fluid. She set these in front of Judas.

He lifted and examined the loaf, took a bite. Well, it seemed safe.

Then another bite, and before he knew it, his awakened ravenous hunger had its way, and the loaf was gone.

The pomegranate was the next item under his scrutiny. No soft spots, cuts, or obvious discolorations...

"Are you going to eat that, or merely stare at it all night?"

Judas looked over apologetically. "Sorry, old habit. It's kept me alive in some difficult situations."

"Oh. Yes, I imagine so. Well, let us resume what we were discussing."

With that, she unwound the head covering and tossed it away from her. The material curled up, seemingly on its own, along the wall between the cushions and the inner door.

Judas didn't notice its odd behavior. He had eyes only for Lilith.

With her head bare, her lustrous black hair tumbled down over her shoulders, gleaming in the fire's light. Her arms and neck, bare and white, peeped through the locks. He had never seen so much—shoulders—on a woman before. It made him wonder what else lay hidden under that black cascade.

The fruit dropped from his hand, forgotten.

Lilith smiled slyly, and slid closer to him. He made as if to pull her to him, but she moved away, her sensuous eyes holding his gaze in a promise he wasn't about to refuse.

A twitch at the side of her mouth. "We must talk."

Judas smiled tightly. "Talk?"

"Yes. There are plans in place for the liberation of Jerusalem from its masters, and my friends and I need your Rabbi's cooperation. Can you make that clear to him?"

Judas' ears perked up. Liberation? Now, that was what he wanted to hear. He wondered what she had in mind.

She continued, "We have friends in authority here, and for quite a while we have wanted Jesus to speak to them. If only he would grant us this favor, just the one time, we could continue with our plans. I do believe you would want to see your people free?"

"Yes! Yes, of course. What is the plan?"

"All in due time." She squeezed his hand, and his heart leapt. As she once again came close, his pulse beat rapidly, and he reached for her.

Although she didn't pull away, she resisted him, but barely.

"I'll need you to do me—that is, us—a favor." Her mouth drew to within inches of his, her breath soft and warm on his face.

"What is it?" Judas whispered, barely able to speak.

She put her hand on his chest, feeling the pounding of his heart. Her eyes widened, and her own breathing quickened.

"Your heart beats so fast. It's very...enticing."

She nuzzled his neck and purred into its curve, "We want you to arrange a meeting between your Rabbi and certain members of the elders on the council."

What? The suggestion jolted him from the feelings he was having.

"No!" Judas pulled back, alarmed at the idea, but not without regret. "That is something I cannot do. That is," he added hastily, not wanting to lose her favors, "I have promised not to do such a thing. We are, as you probably know, out of favor with the Pharisees, who carry a lot of influence. Jesus has asked us not to get involved with the authorities here, which is why we have, as a group, stayed out of the way and to ourselves."

"Until this week." Lilith stared levelly at him.

"Yes..."

"And why was this week different, Judas?"

"I..."

"Perhaps Jesus wants to be known and heard. Perhaps he is just as tired of Roman authority as everyone else. Maybe his recent actions are his way of getting the authorities' attention without involving Roman spies."

Judas considered for a moment. "I hadn't thought of that. Maybe you're right..."

He brightened. This whole week—the donkey, the procession, the scene today in the Temple area—maybe they were Jesus' way of telling everyone that it was time to rise up.

Lilith glanced at the cup.

"You've not had your wine, Judas. Please try it. It's a special mixture I have made especially for myself and my more...special...guests."

A half-smile again, and she held the cup out to him.

Judas took it and looked at the contents. In the shadows cast by the fire, it was difficult to see what its true color was, but sparks of bright crimson danced in its depths when he swirled the cup.

Interesting.

He sniffed at it, and quickly turned his head away. His eyes watered. Such an odd smell! Sweet, but somehow...rancid? Rather like decaying flowers.

He pushed the cup back at Lilith. "No thanks. Um...let me think about what you've proposed, and I can get back to you tomorrow." He was halfway to his feet when Lilith's voice stopped him dead.

"Judas."

Her tone of voice riveted him. It sounded almost menacing, causing fear to rise rapidly from his gut; he realized that he was too afraid to even look at her. Concentrating his gaze on the wall sconce and the fire's warm familiarity, he managed to answer.

"Yes?" He tried to sound casual, but his voice was feeble, shaking.

"I can't let you leave here without your answer. Please, let's have a drink together, and you can give me your answer afterward."

He shook his head, made as if to continue towards the outer door...

...and found himself seated on the cushions again!

He stared wildly around himself in alarm. *How did that happen?*

He made as if to rise again, but found he couldn't move. He quailed as Lilith leaned over him. Her garments parted, and there was no longer any mystery as to what was beneath that long, black hair.

"You do want to stay with me, don't you? I'm sure we can find much in common to...talk about." Her voice was smooth, low, promising.

Judas whimpered, much like Adon had done earlier. Never had he felt so overpowered— and by a mere female!

Lilith purred in his ear, holding the cup towards him again. She turned his face toward her, brushed his lips with hers. Her eyes took over his senses once again. One look, and he fell into the abyss, not caring whether or not he would ever emerge.

The cup was cold in his fingers. He raised the edge to his lips.

"Yes. Drink. It will relax you so that you can think clearly."

The wine entered his mouth. It was as horrid as the smell, but he no longer cared. The taste was salty and coppery, as if he had just put several coins into his mouth.

Then the screaming started. It filled his ears and his brain, blocking out everything...the room, the events of the day, even Lilith herself. He had a mental image of a young man lying on the cushions, a look of terror frozen on his face. Blood ran down his neck from two deep puncture wounds and soaked the pillows. Lilith knelt above the boy, her beautiful face smeared crimson, razor-sharp teeth exposed as she leered at her victim.

Judas screeched in terror. He threw down the cup and scrambled backwards towards the door.

Panting in fear, he turned, jumped up, and was almost through the doorway when he was assaulted by a huge swarm of black gnats. They came out of nowhere, stinging, biting, burrowing into his flesh and flying into his ears and eyes. He swatted at them, screaming and swearing. Breathing became impossible, as they swarmed up his nose and into his mouth.

Judas could feel himself falling into a dark nothingness. Again the screaming, as of tortured souls. He didn't know if the howls came from outside himself or from his own throat. The only thing he was aware of was the screams. Then a hideous laugh, deep and growling, just as he lost consciousness.

The gnats swarmed away from the inert figure, which stirred and stood up. Its eyes were flat, but not dead. It stood as if waiting for instruction.

"You know what to do," said a deep, disembodied voice. "Now go."

Judas walked silently out the door, through the garden, and into the street.

Lilith watched him go. Behind her, the gnats re-formed themselves into a long, sinuous band, and then became the Serpent. It hissed angrily as it wove itself around Lilith's neck and head. "How dare you try to take this one from me," it growled.

Lilith pulled absentmindedly at the serpentine coils. She licked the points of her fangs and smiled longingly at the retreating figure. "I wasn't stealing him from you. I merely wanted a taste."

"You have Adon. That is enough!"

"One is never enough," she retorted, looking the Serpent in the eye. "I want them all."

"What, exactly, did you do to him to make him run away like that?" demanded the Serpent.

"Me? I didn't do anything. All I did was give him his drink. I thought *you* caused him to back away, with some sort of vision or other. I wouldn't put it past you, trying get him away from me."

"It was you and your appetite. I certainly would not have wanted him to leave until I was done with him."

Lilith pouted. "Adon bores me. Always sniffling and whining like a baby. I find that exciting and mouthwatering in the little ones, but in a grown man, it is somewhat disappointing. Maybe I could use a change..."

The Serpent would have none of her complaining. "You will obey my commands, Lilith, or you will pay the consequences. You will get someone new when I decide."

Lilith sighed, went back into the dim recesses of the house, and poured herself a cup of her young servant's blood. She preferred it plain, but the myrrh did add a bit of interest.

The torch, forgotten, sputtered and went out.

CHAPTER 14

Judas moaned and sat up. He rubbed his eyes, then looked around, dazed.

Where am I?

He did not recognize this street. The houses were large, the gardens well-tended.

He found himself in an alley between two homes. On either side, at the ends of the narrow walkway, he could see terraces full of bright, lovely plants and flowers. The enticing odor of cooking wafted past his nose from nearby; obviously the servants were making breakfast for their masters.

Judas' stomach grumbled. Like the prodigal son in one of Jesus' stories, Judas felt as if he would be happy to merely scavenge for the crumbs thrown out for the animals. Considering his lack of finances...

He picked up a rock and threw it in frustration. It landed at the back door of one of the buildings.

"Stop that, you. Get on your way!" shouted someone from the doorway. A meaty-fisted cook scowled at him threateningly.

Judas scowled back, and stood up. He would not be spoken to that way, by a servant or anyone else.

Something fell with a heavy thump at his feet. Startled, he picked it up.

A coin bag? Where did this come from? It was not his! He lifted it, tossed it lightly in his hand. Quite heavy.

The servant had seen it too. His cry of recognition caused Judas to look up at him sharply. The man came at him, his face like a thundercloud, a knife raised in his hand. "Say, you! That is the property of my master. Give that to me. If I didn't despise the so-called authorities in this town, I would drag you to the temple guards. I'd..."

"Mesharet!" The voice rang imperiously from an upper window. Both men looked up.

Mesharet lost his bravado, almost seeming to shrink into himself. An elderly man, his hair flecked with gray, stood at a window. He looked down his aristocratic nose at them.

Mesharet seemed to turn into a different person at the sound of his master's voice. He hunched over, seemingly trying to protect himself.

"Mesharet, this man has my coin purse because I gave it to him."

"I am sorry, Master, I did not know."

Bowing and smiling up at his master, Mesharet backed up once again into the recesses of the house. Not until he was inside again did he turn his eyes away. When he did, he gave Judas a malicious glare, and disappeared into the dark recesses of the room.

The man in the window turned his attention to Judas.

"Why are you still here?" He spoke to the man in the alley as if to a stray dog. "I have paid you well. Now go do as we agreed last night."

Last night?

Judas had no memory of last night, except...

Lilith...

Lilith?

He stood, confused, trying to remember why that name meant something to him. Was it someone he'd met on the street? In the marketplace? A friend of his mother's?

No, he had no recollection of anyone named—what was it? Lily? Lila?

"You!"

Judas jumped, and looked up again.

"Be gone! I don't want to see you until the appointed time."

Judas opened his mouth to ask what he meant, but the older man yelled at him, pointing to the end of the alley.

"Go! Before I set Mesharet on you."

Judas stammered, thought the better of it, and took to his heels. The memory of that huge beast-man with knife raised was enough to send him flying. He'd figure out everything later, in a safer place.

As he got to the street and turned the corner, something the old man had said made him stop in his tracks.

What was that about being paid? Paid for what? He didn't remember doing anything for that man.

A push at his shoulder; two men jostled past. One fixed him with an indignant stare. "Keep moving, you. Your kind isn't wanted around here."

His kind?

Oh, yes. Poor. Right.

Judas sighed. He'd given up his home, his bed, and his inheritance—for what? Couldn't he have simply met up with Jesus when he was passing through, then waved him and his disciples off on the next day? No, he had to wake up in alleys and be spit on by servants.

Grumbling, he sat in the shade of an alcove off the busy street.

Oh! Yes. Now to have a look at what was so heavy in this purse...

He opened it and sucked in his breath, hardly believing what he saw. A glint of silver in the dark recesses of the cloth...Scurrying further out of the public line of sight, he turned out the bag's contents into his lap.

Silver! More than he'd seen since he'd left his home and family behind. He quickly counted his treasure and thrust the talents back into the purse.

Thirty! Well, that more than made up for the money stolen from him the day before. Tying the money-bag firmly to his belt and concealing it deep within his garments, Judas stood.

His heart lighter than it had been in days, he stepped back out onto the street. The marketplace was about to open, and with it the moneychangers' stalls. He'd trade out the silver for ordinary coin, put into another bag the amount taken from him by Barabbas' gang, and keep the rest for himself. He'd been needing new sandals, and it would be nice to pick up something nice for his mother...

Someone seized him from behind. Judas almost screamed, the bandits and their hidden knives in the forefront of his memory.

"Judas!" hissed a familiar voice.

Judas relaxed and turned to his accoster. "Andrew! You almost scared me to death."

"Where have you been? Why did you run out when we were at the temple yesterday? Was it because of the stolen coins?" Andrew looked accusingly at Judas, then eyed the bulge at the side of his waist. "And is this another theft?"

Judas backed away. "No, of course not. I—I went looking for some people I know. Friends. They are secret disciples of the Rabbi. I told them I'd been robbed, and they took pity on me.

They gave me—oh, Andrew, they gave me so much money. You should see!"

Judas opened the pouch. He felt a bit of remorse for lying, but even more for the lovely silver he wouldn't be able to keep for himself now. It couldn't be helped though; he had to save face.

Andrew peered in, and his eyes grew wide. He looked at Judas, astonished. "Who are these people? We should tell the Master, and go to thank them."

Judas flinched at the term "Master". *No one owns me...*Then he smiled. "Well, then, their loyalty to Jesus would no longer be a secret, would it?"

Andrew laughed. "Yes, I guess you're right. Well, come along, we need to find some food to celebrate the Passover."

Judas blinked in surprise. *Passover? Already?*

Andrew sighed. "I do wish you would be a little more observant of what is important. You can't just go through life forgetting who you are."

Judas shook his head and waved away Andrew's gentle reprimand. He certainly had not forgotten. He just didn't act on his faith the way everyone else did. It was...*there*...when it was convenient, and that was fine with him.

Andrew looked over at the shops. Already they were enjoying a busy morning. "We can discuss this another time. Come, let's go buy what we need before all of the best wares are gone!" He pulled Judas with him, and together they made their way through the early crowd. Everyone wanted the very best for their Passover banquets, and the stalls were thronged before the sun was fully over the town.

"Andrew." Judas stopped, looking over at the moneychangers. "We have to get this silver changed to coin so that we can purchase our food."

Andrew grinned and held up a coin bag of his own. "No need. We met a man last night. He gave us not only this money, but a very nice room in the upper floor of his home so that we might observe the Passover comfortably."

Judas' jaw dropped. "When did all of this happen? Two nights ago, we were sleeping against the olive trees in Gethsemane. Last night..."

Wait. Last night? Where did they—did he—lie down to sleep yesterday?

Nothing came to him. He stood, puzzled, trying to remember something. Anything.

Andrew shook him lightly on the shoulder. "Judas?"

He blinked, turned to his friend. "Wha...Oh, I'm sorry. Just...didn't sleep well..."

Andrew nodded, giving Judas a look. "That's right. Your whereabouts." He crossed his arms and regarded Judas from lowered eyelids. "Well, we'll discuss that later as well. Not that your private life is not your own," he added hastily, "it's just that we worry if you, or any of our number, leave and don't tell anyone where you're going."

Judas sighed. *Was Andrew his friend or his mother?* "The room?" he prodded.

Andrew caught his meaning. "Yes. The room. Well, Jesus told a couple of us to wait inside the gates, and follow a man with a water jar…"

Andrew's voice faded as Judas' memory flashed a brief recollection of another water jar, and a weedy garden.

"…and he had it all set up for us." Andrew peered at his companion. His smile disappeared. "Judas? Are you feeling alright?"

Judas brought his concentration back to Andrew with some effort. He smiled. "Yes, of course. Now," he rubbed his hands together, pretending enthusiasm, "let's get to the food before it's gone."

Andrew nodded in agreement, relaxing.

They looked through stalls selling wine and bread, meat, fish, and vegetables domestic and exotic. There were stalls selling herbs and spices from around the known world. At a basket vendor's tent, Judas looked hopefully for a certain young woman bent to the task of her weaving.

However, just a couple of old men, neither of whom he recognized as being Jayla's relatives, shuffled around the small space...

Oh well...

Andrew was at the next tent, testing the firmness of the fruit displayed there. Judas caught up with him, and was about to make a comment when Andrew turned over a particularly ripe fig. It was bruised and open, and a small cloud of flies buzzed up from under it.

Judas gasped and stumbled backwards. He screamed and covered his head and face with his arms.

Shocked, Andrew caught him up and shook him hard. "Judas, what's wrong? Judas!!"

His actions brought Judas quickly back to his senses. He brought his arms down. Onlookers stared at him; the fruit vendor snarled angrily as he cleaned out the offending figs.

"It was only a couple!" the owner cried, trying to convince his prospective customers. "See? The rest are good. I can't help it if the sun bakes holes in perfectly good fruit."

The bystanders went back to their business, shaking their heads and glancing at Judas and Andrew. Poor, crazy man! He should not be allowed out in public, where he could scare normal people.

The fruit vendor shook a stubby, work-worn finger at the pair. "Go! Find your food elsewhere. Such bad business I don't need. I have enough trouble feeding my little ones without your coming around here frightening away my customers."

Andrew and Judas moved off, embarrassed and apologetic.

"Would you please tell me what happened back there?" Andrew hissed.

"I don't...really know. Those flies...they just came at me. I suddenly couldn't breathe. I don't know why." Judas grabbed Andrew's arm, and cried desperately, "Help me, my friend! I don't remember anything from when I left your company yesterday until I woke up this morning."

Andrew stared at him. His concern grew as he realized Judas was not joking. "Come. We have enough provisions. We must go back to Jesus. He'll help you."

The two hurried away from the busy stalls, into the stillness of the quiet side streets.

CHAPTER 15

After meandering through a bewildering number of streets, the two finally stopped at a small side door. It was one of many just like it along that obscure road, but Andrew knew it from the rest.

A man sat on the doorstep, mending a sandal. Judas could not see his face, as the man was wearing a hood that completely covered his head. All he could see was the man's corded, muscled hand as it worked the leather. The man looked up, saw Andrew, and nodded. He regarded Judas with suspicion, but let them through. A flash of metal from under his tunic let Judas know that he was not unarmed.

The two disciples peered through the doorway, and the man returned to his task. Before he entered the house, Judas happened to look back at the dark stranger. He was still sitting in the same place, mending, but something odd caught Judas' eye.

On the man's wrist was an odd, livid scar in the shape of a cross, the skin an angry red. A long-lost memory flashed across Judas' mind: a baby with a cross-shaped light across his body, and a headlong escape into the darkness.

He shook his head to clear it, and followed Andrew into the interior of the house. Up the stairs they went, encountering no one else along the way. The man on the doorstep watched them go. He flexed his scarred hand, rubbing the mark.

The rest of the brothers had laid out the vessels for the Passover, and as one the group prepared the food. The master of the house had sent up a roasted lamb, still warm from the fire. All that was needed was to put out the food that Andrew and Judas had purchased, and to fill the wine cups. Judas got caught up in the camaraderie and forgot about the problems that had been plaguing him.

Jesus sat to one side, watching the proceedings. Judas noticed him, seemingly so sad, and smiled encouragingly at him.

The Rabbi's demeanor bothered him. It was there in his eyes, in the set of his jaw, the way he sat—an overwhelming sorrow, along with an air of finality. Judas couldn't fathom what was so odd about him. It seemed, to him, the way someone would look at the end of a long journey, but without really wanting to see the end of it.

No one else seemed to notice. Judas went back to his task, wondering if he was imagining things.

Soon the preparations were finished, and they began the Passover Seder. Unleavened bread, bitter herbs, wine, the lamb; it looked wonderful. Once the prayers had been said and the rituals observed, the men happily began to serve each other from the dishes on the table. Conversation grew and voices rose, competing to be heard.

Then, a voice louder than all others, although it was not loud in volume, rang out over the rest because it wanted to. Had to. "This night, one of you will betray me."

All action froze. Judas, who was seated close to Jesus, turned to him incredulously.

Betrayal? Who would dare? He looked around at the familiar faces, the men who had become his dearest friends and closest confidantes. How could...how could anyone do such a thing? It was unbelievable.

There was more...

"It is happening as it is supposed to happen, but woe to the man who is the betrayer. Better for him if he had never been born."

The words chilled Judas to the heart, and he could see they had the same effect on the rest of the men present.

Wait. What was it Jesus just said about "it's supposed to happen"? If it's supposed to happen, how can someone be blamed for having done it? Judas, musing on this question, again tried to discern which of these men was the guilty party.

Peter? No, Judas could see him staring steely-eyed at the rest of the group, daring anyone to admit to such treachery.

John?

He looked to Jesus' right side. John was there, the Rabbi's best friend. The two of them were whispering together; John wore the saddest, most bereft look Judas had ever seen.

Well, no one was admitting anything. Judas picked up a piece of bread, absent-mindedly taking a bite as he thought. The bread needed something; Judas never was one for such plain fare. There was a bowl of herbs within his reach—perfect! He was about to dip his bread in the bowl, but the Rabbi got there first by a split second. Their hands collided, and both pieces of bread landed in the herbs.

Judas looked up, smiling apologetically. "Sorry, Rabbi, I..." His voice trailed off.

John looked as if he had seen a monster. Judas looked behind him. *What was that boy scared of?*

He turned back to Jesus, and was transfixed by his gaze. The Rabbi's eyes held sadness and pity. For him? Why?

Judas then heard a voice, Jesus' voice, not in his ears, but in his heart. "What you must do, do it quickly."

John closed his eyes and wept against Jesus' side. Judas looked confusedly at his Rabbi. He shook his head, not understanding.

"Go," the voice said again.

Judas looked at the rest of the men. They were all still busy muttering amongst themselves; it didn't seem as if anyone else had heard. However, John had. Judas could tell by the way he looked at him through tear-filled eyes. Judas stood up slowly, not taking his gaze from Jesus'.

The voice again. This time it was directed to him only; he could tell John was not hearing it. He lay against Jesus, sobbing his heart out. "When you have done what you are going to do, I tell you, do not despair. You are part of the plan of salvation. As such, you must carry out what the Father wills, even if it seems to come from the Evil One. Satan thinks he is causing this, but my Father can make all things right. As I have said, no one will be saved if I am not the One to do it. Keep your faith. Remember what I told you. Go."

Judas looked helplessly around him. The brothers were starting to notice that he was standing. Before they could ask embarrassing questions, he ran out of the room and down the stairs.

He left the house and stood in the deserted street, frightened and confused. Where was he supposed to go, and what was this thing he was supposed to do? In the twilight, he found himself utterly alone. He started walking aimlessly, thought better of it, and stopped.

Maybe if he just sat and thought about what had happened, he could plan his next course of action. It didn't help that he had such a large hole in his memory where last night should have been. Leaning against a wall in a dark side street, he tried to remember just what had gone on after he had fled from those thieves. His memory brought back a few pictures: running down a street, an open gate, hiding, an alabaster cistern...

Suddenly he felt someone watching him. Whoever it was stood just behind him in the gathering dark.

Judas moved slowly, putting his hand inside his cloak and closing it around the hilt of a small dagger. He turned with sudden speed, raised the dagger, and plunged it down...

...into nothingness! At the same time, a woman's laugh rang in his ears. He looked frantically all around himself, but he was alone.

Where was that laughter coming from? There were no windows facing this street, and no one stirred anywhere within his sight.

Frightened, he ran from that street into the main road. Faster and faster he ran, not knowing where he was going. Behind him, a lone individual, hooded and dark, watched him. The cross on the hooded figure's wrist glowed a dull red deep within the recesses of his sleeve. The figure started walking, slowly and deliberately, following Judas' retreating figure.

Judas rounded yet another corner and pounded down the street. Panting, he stopped for a moment to catch his breath. Sides heaving from exertion, he leaned over, supporting himself with his hands on his knees. When he looked up again, he jumped in alarm.

There in front of him were several distinguished-looking men, and behind them a large number of Temple guards. One of the men addressed Judas. "You're on time. Good. Now lead us to him, and be quick about it."

Judas backed away, sweating from both exertion and fear. What did they want? Lead them? *Oh, no...*Cold realization hit him, took his breath away, left him gasping in shock.

Now the mystery of the silver coins was solved, and in the most horrible way Judas could have imagined it.

He was the betrayer! Somehow within the time episode he couldn't remember, he had struck a bargain with these people, whoever they were.

Judas was sick to his very soul. How could he have been a part of this? It wasn't his fault if he had no memory of having done anything. He finally found his voice. "No! I made a mistake. I can't take you to him. I'm sworn to protect his whereabouts."

"You weren't so eager to protect him last night. You even threw rocks at my door to get my attention. Why the change?" Without waiting for an answer, the speaker signaled the Guards, who quickly surrounded Judas.

The captive rolled his eyes madly at the guards. "No, wait! I wasn't myself last night."

The old man, who seemed to be the group's leader, sneered contemptuously. "Then who was it who took my silver and told me he'd meet me here tonight?"

A spear tip touched Judas' back, and he flinched.

"I suggest you take us to your Rabbi, or you will end up in pieces on this street."

The guards grinned, pushing closer to their prisoner.

Judas thought fast. No reason to take them to the Passover room. He could lead them to where he "thought" Jesus would be. He wouldn't be there, and they'd leave him alone. Well, they'd probably let him off with a warning; he was sure he could get away with it.

"Right. Well, no reason to get aggressive." He gave the group a sickly smile.

The spokesman smiled back—a ghastly, evil leer that broke Judas' heart. "I'm glad we agree. Now, please proceed."

The party turned and walked back up the street, first Judas at spear point, then most of the guards. The group of men followed, the rest of the Guards protecting them from behind. Soon the street was again deserted and quiet.

A shadow moved out from between two buildings, then another silent figure from further on. They were joined by a third. The three, all hooded and cloaked, followed the betrayer and his company as they made their way towards the gates of Jerusalem.

Judas was frantically trying to decide where, exactly, he would lead them. It would have to be someplace believable. These people probably already knew most of their hideouts and favorite places.

His thoughts were interrupted by an impatient voice behind him. "Where are you taking us?"

"Just outside the city gates," Judas assured him, hoping he sounded more confident than he felt. "I know exactly where he is."

Judas remembered the Brethren talking about how they would spend the entire evening in that house, and sleep there as well, since the owner had been so kind as to offer his hospitality. They had talked happily about having a warm place, free of dirt and insects, to lay their heads for the first time in many nights.

He found his steps had led him to a very familiar place: the entrance to the olive orchard and garden of Gethsemane. Judas felt a brief pang of fear. What if they had decided to come out here? What could he do then? He listened carefully, and heard nothing but the usual sounds of the nocturnal animals. He sighed in relief. Turning toward the rest, he said, "They are all in here."

"But there are no lights, and I don't hear any voices."

"Well, of course not. What kind of sanctuary would it be if they had light and sound to indicate where they were?" Having said this, and feeling confident that the ruse had worked, Judas entered the garden. The rest followed, the Guards wary and watchful. They walked a long way without seeing or hearing anyone, and after awhile Judas stopped. Turning to the others, he raised his hands and shoulders in a helpless gesture.

"I guess I was wrong. Perhaps they decided to go elsewhere."

"Without telling you?" The spokesman didn't look as if he believed him. "Why would they do that? Aren't you one of them?"

The spear point tickled Judas' back once again.

"Oh, yes! Yes!" Judas hastily reassured him. "But I may have heard wrong. It happens sometimes. I often have to go looking for them elsewhere when I..."

His voice trailed off.

The group was looking over his shoulder, smiles of triumph spreading across their faces.

"Which one is he?"

What? Judas turned slowly, and all life seemed to fly from him.

Jesus and the Brethren were only a short distance ahead of them. He hadn't noticed them because of the dark. The Rabbi stood apart from the rest, and seemed, in the black of night, to be radiating some sort of light around him. His disciples were lying on the ground against the trees, seemingly asleep.

No! Not this! Judas trembled, and he briefly considered the chance he might have of escaping if he just suddenly took off running. Would he get far?

Did it matter? His life was now forfeit. He hadn't known what these men had wanted of Jesus, but he was beginning to understand. These guards had not been brought along to keep *him*, Judas, in check. No, they were here to apprehend the Rabbi! And that meant only one thing: arrest and probably worse.

One more attempt at deception, and it *had* to work.

Judas shook his head. "No, these are not who you're looking for. I don't know them."

"Liar," one of the men hissed. He nodded to the Guard holding the spear on Judas, and the point of it tore through Judas' cloak and tunic. It actually cut him; he could feel blood seeping down his back. He cried out in pain.

"Judas!"came Jesus' voice. He himself had given away his own identity.

"Well? Go. He calls you." The guard laid a hand on Judas' shoulder and pushed him.

Judas moved toward the Brethren.

An idea hit him. Perhaps if he caused a disturbance, the rest of the disciples would wake up, grab hold of Jesus, and make a run for it. They knew this garden well; they could melt into it and be safely hidden within minutes.

He called back to the men and guards in a loud voice, "The man I greet, that is Jesus."

Oh, wake up, brothers. Hide him, for pity's sake!

The Brothers slept on, heedless of the danger. It was as if they'd been drugged. Judas had never seen them so deeply in slumber. They had always been light sleepers, due to the dangers involved in living in the wild. Dangers from more than just the beasts that roamed freely...

Judas strode up to Jesus, pleading silently with his eyes. He made the motions of greeting Him with a kiss. "Rabbi," he whispered, "I have made a huge mistake, and I don't know how it happened. You must wake the brothers and run while you still can."

Jesus looked lovingly at him, and said, "What's done cannot be undone. Leave them come to me. My hour is near." Then Jesus stepped out towards the guards as they marched toward him. "You have come for me. Here I am."

Wonderingly, the guards cautiously took hold of Jesus. They turned and led him back to where the group of dignitaries stood, their eyes shining in triumph.

The disciples stirred. They looked up, first at Judas, then at the backs of the guards leading Jesus away. Shouting, they got up at once and ran after their Rabbi.

All but the two guards that held Jesus turned spears and swords on the angry men. They chased them until they disappeared, then returned to their original order.

Judas watched in misery, and sat down heavily on a boulder. Great, heaving sobs wracked him. He no longer wanted to be alive.

CHAPTER 16

Judas spent an agonized night under the olive trees. No sleep came to give him release, and he wouldn't have welcomed it anyway.

How had this happened? One moment he was in the company of a man who, in his estimation, was the best hope for all of Judea. The next, he had betrayed that same man and sent him away surrounded by soldiers. Now what? There were certainly those in this city who would want Jesus silenced, like John the Baptist before him. Yet what charge could they possibly bring against him?

Judas got up from where he had lain all night, and, brushing himself off, strode back into the city—straight towards where he knew the dignitaries of Jerusalem spent all their waking hours.

They had to listen to him. This was all wrong!

Making his way down a quiet side street on his way to the Temple, Judas was startled to hear the clamor of a rather large crowd. It grew louder as it came nearer, and he was startled to see a dozen or more Roman soldiers turning off the far street and marching straight towards him. He ducked through an open gate leading to a house along the way and waited behind the wall.

Why were so many people out at this time of day? The sun was barely up.

As the soldiers drew nearer, Judas could see a solitary man, dragging a cross, between the soldiers and the noisy throng. Guards behind him prevented the crowd from getting near the prisoner.

Judas sighed, disappointed. Was that all? These crucifixions happened all the time. What was the excitement? He peered closer and gasped, outraged.

Whoever it was they were about to execute, they certainly had tormented the poor man. Judas had never seen anyone so beaten up. His facial features were impossible to identify. And what was that on his head? Thorn branches! Woven into some sort of...crown? What did they mean by this?

Judas' hands clenched in anger. Oh, to have an army at his own back. They would not only free this poor man, they would show the Romans that the Jews they tormented still had a backbone, and they would only take so much.

As the soldiers and their prisoner came closer, followed by scores of people—some wailing, some obviously drunk and making sport of the ordeal—Judas made out a small figure closely following the man carrying the cross.

He froze as he recognized her. It was—*no!*—Jesus' mother! So the beaten-up prisoner was...?

Oh, no...

Judas fell back against the garden wall as the realization sank in. Tears ran down his face.

No! This was not how it was supposed to be. What had he done? It was all his fault. He had led them to him.

Wait...

Jesus could have run, Judas reasoned to himself. Could have done...something. Judas had seen all of those miracles he had performed. Many times, in situations like the one last night, they had all simply walked through the crowds and disappeared.

Not his fault! Judas bit his tongue to keep from crying out. To keep any passersby from noticing him, from dragging him out to add him to the number of victims being disposed of today.

It seemed forever, but finally the last of the crowd went past Judas' hiding place. He watched as they turned the far corner. Sighing, both in relief and regret, he was finally able to look around at his sanctuary.

A weed-choked terrace, a lone door, no windows, and an alabaster water jar...

Terrible memories flitted half-seen through his mind. His heart galloped; he didn't understand the sudden terror, but he knew he had to get out of there. Running back into the street, he rubbed his arms, as if trying to remove some sort of invisible filth. He looked back the way he had come, then toward the Temple area.

He resumed his errand in haste, and was soon at the Temple gate. There were few people within the enclosure, but Judas recognized the one now very familiar face that he was seeking. The old man who had addressed him from a window the previous morning.

"You!" he roared, rushing at the elderly man, who had been deep in conversation with a companion.

The two temple priests looked at this maniac in alarm and tried to run away. Judas seized his quarry and spun him around. He yelled into the man's face, "What is the meaning of this? What have you done? Jesus is innocent of—why is he being crucified?"

The priest stared in terror into Judas' half-mad eyes. He tore himself away. "What did you think our intent was?" he snarled angrily. "This Jesus of yours is a threat, not just to the Jewish leaders, but to everything we know and cherish. The Romans would have seen him as a threat eventually..."

"'Eventually'?" Judas was aghast. "Then it was not the Romans' idea..."

"No. We had to persuade Roman authority to see it our way. We made up a few things, paid off a few people...," here the old man smiled slyly, "including you, I'd remind you."

Judas froze at the reminder. All courage left him, and once again he realized the horrific part he had played in Jesus' death sentence.

The priest and his companion noticed. They smiled conspiratorially at each other. "I might even go so far as to say that, without your cooperation, this may not have come to such a beneficial conclusion."

Judas fingered the silver in the pouch at his waist. Rage such as he had never known rose up within him, engulfing his senses. With a mighty roar, he leapt on the two priests, fists flying. He hardly knew what he was doing. All went black in his mind. He felt nothing but blind fury.

The next thing he knew, he was standing within the Temple itself...and not in the public area. Somehow he had found his way into the Holy of Holies, forbidden to all but the priests, and was before the altar of sacrifice.

Judas knew he shouldn't be here. He knew some sort of reverential awe should have taken over his very being. From his childhood, he knew what the Holy of Holies was.

The very Presence of God to His people.

Yet where had this God been when Judas had needed Him? Why hadn't He saved Jesus from this fate? Jesus had said that it was supposed to happen this way, but how did he know? Maybe he had been mistaken, had not seen his own death coming for him in Gethsemane.

Why was he, Judas, suddenly the pivotal reason Jesus was going to be destroyed?

Why, God? WHY???

He fell to his knees, not in reverence, but because his anger had taken away all ability to stand or do anything else. It pulled in all of his energy, absorbed it into a black core within him. All of his being was now concentrated into an almost living entity of pure hatred.

With an animal scream, Judas tore the pouch of silver from his belt and threw it with all of his might straight at the altar. The coins flew and scattered everywhere. At the noise, several priests ran in to see what was going on. They stopped, shocked, to see a man splayed on the marble floor of that most sacrosanct of places.

Judas bellowed again.

"NO!"

The outcry echoed to the ceiling with desperation. Judas burst into tears, his fists clenching and unclenching. Then, before the astonished priests could get their bearings, he was on his feet and away.

Judas didn't stop running until he was well away from the Temple precincts. He walked, dazed, not knowing or caring where he was going. His tears blinded him, as did his fury. He found himself near the main gate leading out of the city. The crowd was out there at the foot of a small hill known as Golgotha; shouting, crying, all of them making themselves heard, either for or against the organized legal murder of this good man.

Then the sounds of hammering, the muffled, unmistakable sound of nails through flesh. Women shrieking, men shouting.

Judas could not shut it out. He ran, but the sound followed. It chased him through the deserted marketplace, echoed back at him from the high walls of the city, seemed to mock him in the streets.

Laughter now. Evil, triumphant laughter, which drowned out the sounds of crucifixion.

Judas looked around wildly. Where was that laughter coming from? There was no one around but a few hardy vendors, who sat idly selling to no one, waiting for the crowd to get bored and come back in to buy their wares. They calmly went about their day as if nothing was different.

Didn't they hear the laughter?

Judas noticed that they had suddenly taken a great interest in him. One pointed at him and said something in a low voice to another, who nodded. They both peered more closely at him.

Judas understood all too clearly. They knew him as one of Jesus' hand-picked disciples. Was there a price on his head too? Were they willing to sell his whereabouts to the highest bidder? Judas backed out of the public square, ran out of the city through a small side door, and didn't stop until he was outside the walls. He made his way to a cave across a small plain, far away from any prying eyes.

He stood, winded, behind a boulder that partially blocked the cave's entrance. Alone with his hopelessness and despair, he slid down to the cave floor, put his head on his knees, and wept.

He was unaware of the passage of time. The lack of sound from outside woke him from a fitful sleep.

Looking out from behind the boulder, he was dismayed to see that he had an unobstructed view of the grisly proceedings outside the gates of Jerusalem. Much of the crowd had dispersed, leaving only a few citizens and a handful of soldiers. The sky had turned an ominous shade of greenish-black, bruised and violent. Clouds swarmed and roiled over each other, and lightning flew through and between them.

How long had Jesus been on that cross? Was he still alive? Judas couldn't see how; when he'd seen Jesus in the street with that heavy wood, it seemed he had barely enough strength to stand. His clothes had been soaked red, and his face had been covered with the blood seeping out of the wounds caused by those horrid thorns.

Judas closed his eyes, trying to shut out both the scene before him and the memory of that blood-stained face.

A cry reached his ears. His eyes flew open, unable to stay closed. His gaze moved against his will to the figure on the cross.

Jesus' voice could be heard across the distance to the cave.

Across space and time, past and future, changing everything, proving everything:

"It is finished..."

A cry of pain, of love...of triumph.

Judas felt the earth rock, saw boulders skitter and split across the field. He ran from the cave, fearing that the roof would fall in on him, barely able to keep his footing.

Screams came from inside the city. In terror, Judas watched as numerous mists rose from the ground, forming into human shape, walking through the very walls of Jerusalem.

What was this he was seeing?

The earth continued to shake, and as Jesus bowed his head in death, a great shimmering sphere of energy seemed to tear out of his very being. It grew, reaching for the heavens, enveloping the earth.

And Judas knew, without knowing how he knew:

The God of the Universe, the Ancient of Days, the true Holy of Holies, the Creator of all, was no longer being held within Jesus' body. He was free, and the world could not hold Him. God Himself, born into humanity, had returned to Who He Was.

Judas was stunned, both at the scene before him, and what he could not deny. He sat, unmoving, and stared out toward the cross.

Suddenly, a cold chill ran down his spine, and the hairs on the back of his neck stood on end. There was a presence beside him. An unearthly being. Terrified, Judas turned his head slowly to see what was now inexplicably beside him.

He gasped and scrabbled away, then stopped, amazed at what he saw.

It was his father!

The ghost of Simon Iscariot stood not five feet away from him, staring at him silently.

CHAPTER 17

Judas rubbed his eyes. "Father?" he asked, incredulous.

The specter nodded his head.

Judas blinked. His father. Alive again! At least he looked alive. No, wait, it was still possible to see the outlines of things behind him.

A ghost! Like all of those other mists that had appeared at the time of the earthquake. Judas cowered, unable to move.

Simon spoke, and his voice had an echoey, distant sound to it. "Judas. My son."

"How? But—but..."

"Have no fear of me. I have been sent to help you."

"Help me?" Judas was almost gibbering in fear.

"Yes. I have come to tell you not to despair. Your part in these events was crucial to God's plan of salvation."

"My part?" Fear was turning quickly to rage, as the unfairness of it all returned to him in all its horror. "*My* part? Why was I not asked if

I even *wanted* to have a part in this?" His eyes flashed in anger as he sat on the ground, glaring at his father's shade.

Simon looked levelly into his son's eyes. "Would you have carried out your part if you had known?"

"Yes!" Judas bellowed, tearing up the grass beside him in rage.

Simon waited calmly. After a moment of silence, Judas dropped the clump he had been holding. He stared miserably at the ground. "No..." he muttered.

Simon nodded once, slowly. "And because you knew nothing, and helped bring about the events of today, the Scriptures have been fulfilled. We dead walk among the living this hour to prove we still exist, and that we have been freed from Sheol."

Simon looked heavenward, joyous, and raised his arms toward the sky.

Judas peered at his father. There seemed to be a glow about him that hadn't been there at first. "Father? If you are no longer in Sheol, where will you go? Do you return to us?"

Simon's smile was beatific. "No, my son, we go to the abode of the Father. We will see Him face-to-face and be with him eternally."

Judas was amazed. It had come to pass! That which God's people had been hoping for all these centuries had finally happened.

"But...did Jesus have to die?"

"Yes, son. It is all written in the Scriptures. You must have eyes and heart to see it."

Even though this was joyous news, Judas' heart was still soured against having been the means by which one of his best friends had been destroyed. He had no intention of ever looking at Scripture, or entering a synagogue again. If he wasn't imagining things—that the dead were finally free and salvation set forth for all—the revelation was beyond wonderful. However, the horrifying truth of betrayal remained.

A new thought entered his mind. What if he was imagining this whole conversation? He was exhausted; he could be seeing things...

Then he remembered something terrible.

"Father! Jesus said that it would have been better for me if I had never been born. What does that mean? Am I condemned?" The rage resurfaced. "It was God's idea, not mine! How can I be damned for all eternity for something I knew nothing about?"

"This crisis in your heart is why I am here. Jesus said not to despair. Forgive yourself. Do not let yourself be overwhelmed by human emotions. Look beyond the present and see the world's salvation. You have a hard road ahead of you because of what has happened, but you are not beyond redemption."

Judas focused on the words that enraged him and ignored the rest. "Forgive myself? I just said I had nothing to do with it."

"You did, though. Maybe not directly, but the way you have lived your life, concentrating on what you wanted instead of looking toward the good of others, set you up for the Tempter's work. Even so, God has used your weakness to accomplish His will.

"You would not have been in that garden with Satan's...companion...if you had remained with your brothers. You knew better in your heart even before you sought Barabbas, but you did not act on it."

"Wait." Judas held up his hand, confused. "What 'companion'?"

"The woman. Lilith."

Then Judas remembered. The garden. The woman's wiles. Their conversation. How he had wanted her.

The coppery-tasting wine. The...boy...in that vision he had had. Lilith, her face bloodied. The flies that had engulfed him, and no knowledge of anything else until the next morning...

Simon spoke again, gently. "That is when Satan took you over, my boy. You were not strong enough to fight him. Because of how you lived, you were vulnerable to his mastery over you. And he will use your anger to use you again, to own you if he can."

"What do you mean? I serve no master but myself!" Judas spat the words at his father.

"And that is why you fall."

The light around Simon shimmered. He looked up again, then at his own hands. They were engulfed in brightness. "I am going now, Judas. Remember what I said. Pass from this despair and rage. Forgive. Be forgiven. Accept God's will for you, and do not give in to the Devil. Be with me some day."

Judas reached toward his father, panicked. He tried to hold onto Simon's garments, but his hand passed through them. "Father!" he cried desperately. "I want to go with you now! I don't want to be here on my own!"

The evening twilight answered him with silence. The light was gone, and so was Simon Iscariot.

Judas stumbled blindly towards the city walls. His desolation engulfed him in a fog of despair.

Forgive? Who? How? Himself? There was nothing to forgive. Was there?

Yes. Maybe. He hadn't lived his adult life the way he'd been brought up. He didn't see where it was worse than anyone else's, though. He had always been in control, always his own master.

Forgive God? God was supposed to be perfect and all-knowing. Forgiveness would mean He had made an error. Or was he looking at it the wrong way?

It suddenly occurred to him in a different light.

Forgive...life.

He stopped walking to think about this new idea. To forgive life meant to let go of the past, and leave these events in God's hands, knowing by faith that He is in control. Not to let the past own you, but to ask for His strength, and to move on. To say "yes" to Him, because He knew what He was doing, even if it made no human sense at the moment.

In a flash, it was crystal-clear to Judas. A burden lifted from his heart, and he walked with more of his usual confidence.

He mulled these thoughts over as he approached the gates.

Other thoughts crept in, thoughts of a more present nature. Such as, where to lay his head for the night. There was no way he could go back to the brothers, at least until their anger against him had subsided. He hoped that the revelation he himself had gotten would also be revealed to them. He'd wait until he could reason with them, and relate all that had happened to have caused this tragedy-turned-triumph.

Just before the gate was a small encampment. The campfire flickered on two people enjoying its warmth. Judas was about to pass them by, when a glint of gold sparked and caught his attention. He stopped and turned toward the camp, his heart fluttering.

Could it be?

He held his breath, waited for another movement.

That glint of gold. It twinkled off the woman's headdress, reflected in the firelight.

Jayla! Judas grinned widely and strode over to where she sat, plaiting reeds by the fire's glow.

It had to be her. The same stance, the deft handling of her craft, even how she bent her head as she worked. He was about to hail her, when she looked up and lIfted the veIl.

Judas froze, stifling a scream. Lilith looked out from beneath the scarf, her eyes maliciously triumphant, her smile scorning him. "Oh, Judas," she purred, "what have you done?"

Judas backed away, too frightened to run. Lilith stood and was at his side all in an instant, leaning on him, speaking low into his ear. He found himself immobile in her grasp.

A smile lifted one side of her mouth. "So, you remember everything about our little 'meeting'. Oh well, I suppose it couldn't be helped." She raised her hand to Judas' face and caressed it. Judas couldn't breathe; he stared in terror at her fingers against his cheek.

Talons! Long and horrid—inhuman!

Judas broke free of her embrace and stumbled backwards. Turning to run, he fell over the other figure by the campfire. The man's face was inches from his own, and Judas could see by the light of the fire that something was terribly wrong.

Lilith's companion was dead!

Judas pushed himself up and away, causing the corpse to roll toward the flickering light. The poor man's throat was torn, blood clotting on two deep gouges scored from his chin to his chest.

Judas was petrified, horror growing as Lilith neared him again. She looked down at her victim and licked her claws. She gave the dead man a little kick, and looked up at Judas. "He annoyed me," she said with a shrug. Then she bent down and wiped the coagulating blood off the dead man's throat, putting her red, sticky fingers into her mouth. She looked up at Judas and smiled widely, her tongue protruding slightly between her fangs.

A long, loud scream pierced his ears. It took Judas a moment to realize that the sound came from his own throat. He ran madly into the night, back the way he had come, and didn't stop until he found himself hiding behind a large tree way beyond the lights of the city. Hoping that that...*she-creature*...hadn't followed him, he sat with his back against the rough bark, his whole body trembling.

He had to get away from here, but with no money, how far would he get? The Brethren wouldn't help him, even if he managed to get back into the city. What chance did he have of not being recognized and brought to trial, simply for being a follower of Jesus? The citizens and guards were looking for all of them, he was sure, and Judas had no idea where the other disciples were.

And there was still the possibility of Barabbas' men hunting for him...

"You're in quite a mess, aren't you?" The voice was right in his ear. Screeching, Judas jumped up and sprinted away, seemingly all in the same motion.

Now she was in front of him!

"No!" Judas gasped. He stopped and tried to turn from her, but her eyes locked on his and he couldn't move. He stood transfixed as her eyes got blacker and blacker. She moved sinuously toward him, leering evilly. "Judas, be realistic. Your Jesus is dead, and you helped kill him. Your friends will consider you a pariah, and will never take you back. You can't return to your previous life, you have no way of going elsewhere..."

Her version of the truth clouded his mind. All of those hopeful thoughts of redemption he had had earlier were erased. Desolation penetrated his very bones, and tears ran down his cheeks. Still he remained immobile, pinned to the spot by her gaze.

"Your only choice," Lilith crooned, "is to come with me. I can promise you a new life, away from any cares, where you can be more powerful than you have ever imagined."

Power. Freedom. Yes...

The memory of his father suddenly pushed away what Lilith was saying. A phrase, which Judas clung to like the last plank of a sinking ship: 'The mercy of God.'

Yes! He would have nothing to do with Lilith or her promises. He tore his eyes away from her hypnotic stare. "No! I won't! I'll kill myself first."

"Is that so?" Lilith's voice was mocking. "I doubt it. You have always been weak. It would be impossible for you to do violence to yourself. There is too much love for your own skin. And what of your Lord and Master? He rather frowns on someone taking his own life."

Judas flushed with anger. "If it means getting away from you, I'll do it. If God doesn't take my life from me to save me from your evil, I have no choice."

Lilith laughed, her sharp fangs glinting in the moonlight. Judas quailed at the sight, and turned away. When he did, he saw a large, long rope tied around the tree he had hidden behind. Odd, he hadn't noticed it before. He strode over, untied the rope, and fashioned a noose out of it. Flinging the other end over a high branch, he quickly clambered up the trunk and out onto the limb.

Lilith watched, amusement in her eyes.

Glaring defiantly at her, Judas tied the rope around the branch, put the noose around his neck, and rolled off the branch.

Death did not come quickly. In fact, to Judas' surprise, it didn't come at all.

Swinging at the end of the rope, his feet brushing the ground, he wondered dully when the light of life would go out, and he would be with his father again. Then, to his horror, the rope around his neck grew ice-cold. The rough cord turned into a dry smoothness, which seemed to twine with a life of its own.

He looked at the rope stretched above him, and gaped at what he saw.

The rope had become...a serpent! A huge, black snake, blacker than any shadow could ever be. Its red eyes regarded him coldly as it wound its coils tighter around Judas' neck.

The terrified man kicked the air, pulled at the loathsome reptile. He clawed and beat at the indifferent scales. The Serpent looked over at Lilith, who quivered with excitement. Judas' eyes unwillingly followed its gaze. His heart, his breath, everything stopped at the sight.

Lilith floated towards him, actually *floated*, and stood before him as he tried to free himself.

He fought like a fly caught in a web, but his struggles had no impact on the Serpent.

Lilith looked up at the snake. It spoke two words: "Take him."

It dropped Judas, but before he could move, Lilith had him pinned against the tree. With inhuman speed, she had her fangs buried in his throat.

The pain! The helplessness! She laughed while she sucked out his blood, sated herself on every drop in his body. Judas gave a cry, and slumped to the ground, lifeless.

Lilith stood looking down on him, a satisfied smile on her face. The Serpent slithered down the trunk of the tree and lay on Judas' chest, regarding the dead man. All at once, it struck, shooting its venom into Judas' chest. When it finished, it wound its way into the night.

"He is ready. You know what to do."

Lilith watched her master as he disappeared into the night, and nodded. From nowhere, she produced another rope, and quickly hung Judas' body back up in the tree. Sated, and gorged on Judas' blood, she disappeared. The new day would come soon enough, and with it the next step in their plans.

CHAPTER 18

Judas opened his eyes in total darkness. He was lying on cold stone, and the silence was absolute.

He sat up. There was a dull ache around his throat, and he was only dimly curious as to why. Gradually his senses awakened, every one of them sharper than he had ever known them to be. The totality of the darkness gave way to a multitude of phosphorescent lights, some more brilliant than others. One glowed strongly near his hand; he reached over and touched it.

It felt like human skin, but very cold to the touch. He explored further with his fingertips; here an arm, there a rib.

This was a human corpse! Judas pulled his hand away, shocked and frightened. Looking around quickly, he realized with growing terror that the rest of these...things...were also dead bodies.

What am I doing in here? I'm not dead.

He jumped to his feet, teetered at a sudden loss of strength, and collapsed back down onto the corpse. Rolling off, disgusted, he came face-to-face with another. Bellowing in fright, he pushed himself clear and stood again, although shaking with the effort.

There had to be a way out! Where was the entrance? This place seemed to be a catch-all for dead people, from the haphazard way these bodies were dumped. Bodies of the homeless, the unclaimed, the unwanted, *the crucified*, suicides...

That thought stopped him short. He put his hand to his neck, exploring the rope burns, and remembered...

The memories were faint, but he knew he hadn't died by hanging. Had he? No, he was certain of it. Further exploration brought his fingers to two huge holes in the side of his neck.

It was Lilith, and that monstrous snake! Judas rubbed his arms, his face, his chest. He felt for his own heartbeat, afraid of what he might—or might not—find.

It was there, but so faint. How could he be alive after what she had done to him? His thoughts were interrupted by the whisper of rodent feet. Rats, coming to feed on the dead. His hearing, also extremely acute, could pick out where they were and how many.

The odor of life, of living blood, engulfed him. A ravening hunger came on him, and he followed his senses to where a large rat was gnawing on a disembodied leg. To Judas, the animal glowed a rich, irresistible crimson red.

With speed he didn't know he possessed, Judas raked up the huge rodent. One powerful shake, and the rat was dead, its neck broken.

Judas held the creature, staring at it. He felt nothing for it, just curious as to why he had done such a thing. Warm, sticky fluid dripped down his arm. The result of his shaking had partially severed the animal's head, and its blood oozed from the wound.

Greedily, Judas licked his arm clean, the sweet, sickly taste a feast to his senses. Overcome with bloodlust, he drained the rest of the blood from the dead creature. Then he threw the carcass down and scented for more of its kind.

Kicking through the piles of human corpses, Judas found himself back to where he had awakened. The glow from the body he'd briefly examined earlier was growing dim. Curious, Judas put his hand on the man's chest again.

A very faint, very slow heartbeat, very likely undetectable by anyone with normal senses. Judas could feel the blood moving sluggishly in the veins below the surface of the skin. The blood lust took him again, and he scrabbled at the dead man's torso and limbs, trying to open a passageway to slake his thirst.

Just then he heard footsteps approaching from outside. He scrambled up, hiding himself in a crevasse in the cave's wall, and waited. The stone over the entrance moved aside, seemingly on its own. Three forms stood silhouetted in the late evening's light.

Judas jumped from his hiding place, snarling, and leapt on the closest of his intended victims. To his utter surprise, his intended quarry snarled back. They wrestled and rolled on the ground, each trying to tear the other's throat out. Judas ended up being pinned down by the other within a few minutes.

The stranger sat on him; now he was the predator and Judas the prey. The man snarled again, showing long, sharp fangs. Judas gaped, recognizing who this abomination used to be.

The servant boy, Adon.

The transformation was incredible. All fear, all human winsomeness and innocence, was gone. In their place was a demonic creature, human in appearance but in reality an undead servant of the Devil...and it looked for all the world as if Adon would soon be finishing him off.

Judas struggled, but because of his loss of blood, he was too weak to escape. Adon snarled again, and clamped an iron hand around Judas' throat.

"Enough!" ordered a voice like dark thunder. It came from one of the other two, neither of whom had moved a muscle. They stood watching, their expressions impassive.

The thing that had been Adon reluctantly let Judas go, and, standing up, walked back to the others.

Judas peered at Adon's companions, not really surprised to see that one of the trio was Lilith. She smiled and held out her hand to him. "Judas, do come and join us."

So very like those words spoken so long ago, uttered by...

"No!" That thunderous voice again. He looked in surprise at the dark, hooded figure standing next to Lilith. "He will not help you, so do not think you will be saved. You are mine, as is Lilith, the boy here, and the souls of any I care to destroy."

Judas looked from him to Lilith. She glanced at the black specter beside her. "Come to me, Judas. You are in need of sustenance if we are to travel tonight."

"Who are you?" Judas ignored her, and directed his question to the hooded one.

"I am Lucius. That is all you need to know for now."

Judas was about to ask another question when a movement caught his eye. A sheep was tied to a tree nearby, grazing peacefully. His breath came heavily as a red mist coated his vision.

"It is yours. Take it," Lilith said.

"What?" Adon raged. "You said I could have it. Where is mine?"

Lilith glared at Adon, visibly annoyed. "Go find something yourself, you miserable, spoiled child. I'm tired of doing everything for you.

"Judas has to have this. Don't you remember when you first woke? How hungry you were? Tonight we move off, and Judas must be strong enough to travel." She turned back to where Judas had been, but he had already started toward the sheep.

The creature lifted its head, scented trouble, and tried to run away. It got to the end of the tether and, because it didn't know any better, kept pulling in the same direction, strangling itself as a result.

Judas caught the sheep up and scraped at its wool, trying to break open its skin. He threw it on the ground and went after its belly, trying to rake it open with his ineffectual human fingers. He cried out in frustration as the animal's wool kept him from making any progress.

"Judas, wait." Lilith was right beside him. She pushed Judas away gently, and, with one swipe of her talons, tore a hole in the sheep's throat.

Judas fell on it, gorging himself on the blood that flowed from the open vein. Finally, he sat back, smeared with gore. Now he could feel true strength through his own veins, a physical power he had never known before.

"How are you feeling?" asked Lilith.

Judas just grinned.

Lilith smiled with pleasure. "Wait until you've fed on your first human. There is nothing like it."

Judas glanced at Adon.

Hmmm...

"No, Judas. Adon has already been awakened. You will have to seek others." Lilith sounded a little disappointed. Adon sneered and turned away.

Spoiled brat, Judas thought to himself.

The sound of something heavy hitting the ground caught their attention.

"What?" Lilith gasped. "I thought we were alone out here."

"We were," intoned Lucius. "They arrived while you were distracted with feeding your newest acquisition."

Lilith didn't favor him with a reply. She pointed up a slight rise to the west, where a group of darkly-clad figures could be seen. They were busily engaged in something that took all their attention.

Dashing from shadow to shadow, the four managed to get close enough to watch the activity. About a dozen people were working on a cross which lay on the ground. It had not been cut down; someone had pulled it out of the hole in which it had been set. Ropes lay on the ground, still tied to the crossbeam. The workers were breaking the cross into small shards and carrying the pieces away in baskets.

One of them pried loose a piece of parchment that had been affixed to the topmost part of the cross. He read it slowly, put it to his lips in reverence, and put it into his tunic. His actions caused his sleeve to slip, exposing his forearm. Judas could plainly see a glowing shape scarred into the man's wrist; a cross, which stretched to his elbow.

Lilith and Lucius had seen it as well. They growled and hissed, backing away, pulling Judas and Adon with them.

"Hunters!" Lucius spat.

"How did they get here? I thought we'd destroyed them all in Egypt," Lilith gasped.

"Apparently not. This means that time is now of the essence. We must go..."

"Adon!" Lilith interrupted, pointing. Her servant was charging up the hill, mad with hunger.

She started up after him, but Lucius stopped her. "No. He will do as he will, and we will see the outcome." Lucius spoke quietly, watching.

At least it seemed as if he were watching. Judas peered at the dark man. His face was odd, its features hard to distinguish, like the faces in dreams.

Adon, bloodthirsty and eager to prove himself, ran without caution towards a lone figure toting a basketful of splintered wood. His intended victim turned, yelled a warning to his fellows, and pulled a sharp piece of the cross from his basket. As Adon came on, fangs bared, the man stood fearlessly, head raised high. He stared at the vampire rushing at him, muttered a few words, raised his eyes to the heavens, and waited.

Adon jumped at him, seeing the wood far too late to stop the inevitable collision. Wood met chest, plunged through, and then out Adon's back. The vampire howled, convulsed, and, to everyone's amazement, exploded into dust.

Everyone's amazement but Lucius'. He looked on patiently, an air of triumph about him.

A silver mist swirled up from the dust heap that had been a poor, misused servant boy. At the same time, black forms began to swirl around the disembodied soul. Lucius grunted, laughed in his throat.

Suddenly the laugh of triumph turned to a howl of dismay and rage, as two fiery orbs appeared out of nowhere. They beat back the blackness and took hold of Adon's soul.

"No!" Lucius stormed up the hill. "He is mine! I destroyed him! His soul belongs to me!"

"Adon was misled," came a voice from the direction of the orbs. "He was deceived by you, plunged into evil. Because of his weakness, and the ills that plagued him in his life, he was easily swayed. The Master, in His great mercy, has granted him forgiveness, and he will be with his True God for all eternity."

Judas ran towards the orbs, desperate. "Take me, too! I cannot bear to have this evil happen to me. Please!" he cried, tears smearing his vision.

A gentle voice, soft as spring rain. "You despaired of God's mercy, Judas. Your betrayal of His Son is not what keeps you from the glory of Heaven. It is your unwillingness to part with your pride. The taking of your own life in defiance of His Will is what keeps you rooted to this life. Here you must stay until such time as you have bent your own will to His, emptying yourself of your pride."

The orbs surrounded Adon's soul and transported it away, into the velvet night sky. Judas swore he could hear faint singing above him. He stood quietly, tears running down his face, staring up at the stars.

Lucius roared, a sound that caused the earth to tremble. And Judas realized with terrible clarity that here stood not a man at all.

Before he could attempt an escape, Lilith grabbed the hapless man, pulling him down the hill. Lucius followed, holding the Hunters back with a look so demonically terrible that the men could not move.

As the night wore on, the three made their way north, to the sea, and to a land where they hoped that the Hunters would not find them.

They moved swiftly over the countryside, snatching up the occasional sheep, or shepherd, as the mood struck them.

At least Lilith and Judas did. Lucius had no need to join them in their feedings. He waited and kept watch as the other two worked over a fresh kill. Lilith had to help Judas, as he was not fully turned yet. Judas abhorred his bloodlust, and despised the company he was forced to keep, but he couldn't work out a plan of escape with the pace they were keeping. Lucius, being who—and what—he was, could fly as swiftly as the spring winds behind them.

The sun was just beginning to rise above the eastern horizon when they caught sight of its light on the sea. The trio quickly found shelter in an abandoned shepherd's cave.

At least it became abandoned after they'd sated themselves on the shepherd...

Lilith curled up in a dark corner, wrapping her cloak around her head and face. Soon she was like the dead. Lucius sat close to the entry, waiting and watching.

Judas paced the cave's floor, his nerves still jangled from all that he had experienced in the past couple of days. Occasionally he would glance over at the dark figure staring out at the world from his post, just outside the reach of the sunlight. Even in the light of day, Lucius' features were indistinct. Not that Judas wanted to look at him for any length of time. He felt that madness lay in that direction. He only knew that Lucius was watching him constantly, even when his head was turned. It unnerved him, that eyeless stare beneath that black cowl.

Suddenly Judas could stand it no more. In an instant, he had rushed past Lucius and was at the entrance to their hiding place. What did it matter what either of them did to him? Perhaps they would kill him, let his soul escape and go...where?

He'd think of that later.

Judas had one foot into the sunlight, and was about to dash out of the cave's mouth, when a shadow suddenly surrounded him. He found himself immobile, as if Lucius had somehow swallowed him whole. The memory of the flies seized him, terrified him. He tried to call out, but couldn't make a sound.

Then, just as quickly, the shadow was gone. Judas, gasping for breath, dared to look behind him. Lucius sat where he had been before. A low, evil laugh surrounded Judas' mind, and then Lucius' voice: "On second thought, go ahead. Leave. Or at least try. What do I care? You're Lilith's pet, not mine."

Judas wasted no time, did not stop to consider what Lucius meant. Not believing his fortune, he bolted out into the morning sunshine—and was immediately seared by the light of day.

He screamed, fell, writhed on the ground, bloody foam at the corners of his mouth. The sun beat down on him, the light of the living cursing the appearance of the undead. Judas could feel his skin drying, blackening, sloughing off as he became dust. He was vaguely aware of another's screams—a woman's.

Mother?

Then the darkness enveloped him again, and he felt himself transported back into the cave.

He passed out.

When he came to, Lilith was kneeling over him. He had a sudden sharp memory of his vision of Adon, and fearfully raised a hand to his throat. His mouth was dry, his eyes on hers, fearing the worst yet somehow hoping for it.

Lilith put her hand on his cheek. "No, dear Judas, I haven't done anything...else...to you."

Judas shuddered, tears misting his vision. He turned away from her touch. Despair seized his heart. Would he ever be rid of these two?

Lucius spoke from his corner. "It is time to complete his awakening. Yet, even so, he is too weak, too...human...to accompany us. We will have to leave him here to fend for himself."

Lilith looked over, shocked and hurt. "What? No, he's...you said..."

"Yes. Your 'first-born', as you've referred to him. But you forget, you still carry your first child within you."

She glared at him. "Please try to recall your promise to my Master when you took his place at my side..."

He sighed. "Very well, he may remain with us, but he is *your* headache; if the Hunters catch up with us, I will abandon both of you."

Judas became more and more frightened as he listened to this conversation. He tried to get up, to make another attempt at freedom, but found that he was once again immobile.

Lucius noticed his struggles. "Mortal man, do you not know, even now? Surely you understand who I am. You cannot be that blind. There is no escape. Your God will not take you back, cursed as you are. I am now your Master."

Through clenched teeth, Judas managed to bellow, "I HAVE NO MASTER!"

Lucius sighed again. "Get it over with. I tire of this conversation," he told Lilith.

Lilith gazed down somewhat dreamily at the man on the ground. She ran her hand slowly down the side of his face, traced the throbbing pulse in his throat with her finger. Judas shook with fear, and his heart hammered. Her eyes blackened as she felt his racing heartbeat; a small smile played on her lips, her breath coming faster.

She suddenly grabbed his chin, pushed his head up, and buried her fangs in his throat. Judas moaned, unable to cry out. After draining his life fluids, she pulled away. This time Judas remained conscious, curious as to how this could be. Certainly he had to be dead.

She put her lips to his, and he could taste his own blood.

Smoke issued from her mouth, and flowed directly into his body. Judas' eyes widened in fear. What was this new horror? He fought as best as he could, but the force was stronger. This was far worse than the bites had ever been. Something living was embedding itself into his very being, taking over space, mingling with his very essence.

He had a vision of a young man, muscled, thick-boned, wearing nothing but a loincloth made of goatskin. He smiled at Judas with an evil smirk, and then the vision was gone. And so was Judas...

Cain's soul looked out at the world through Judas' eyes.

CHAPTER 19

It only lasted a moment, then the struggle began. The two souls locked in battle for supremacy of the body they now both inhabited.

Lilith watched, amused, as the facial features formed and re-formed, first as the more recent visage of Judas, then as the rough, primal face of Cain, then back to Judas again. The body writhed, the mouth screamed in silent agony as the battle went on.

"Enough!" Lucius barked. "I am tired of this lunacy. Animal!" he screamed at the monster that used to be Judas. "You will obey my commands. Judas will be alpha, since he knows this time and world around him. Cain will stay in the background and learn. You will be known from now on as Bestias."

The creature glared at Lucius, both souls hating the name. "No!" they roared in unison.

"You WILL obey me!" Lucius and his monster glared at each other, each trying to outdo the other in both supremacy and contempt.

Then Lucius laughed, low and sinister. "Oh, that's right. I forget. You 'have no master'".

He turned away, starting towards the city. "That's what my brothers and I told the Creator. Hmmm...good start to your career."

The monster stared after him. Lilith looked at her offspring before she, too, turned towards the coastal city of Tyre. "Come along—*Bestias*."

He followed grudgingly, not knowing what else to do.

The three of them entered the city gates as twilight overtook day. They made their way to the harbor, where several Roman merchant ships sat at anchor. After secreting themselves in an alleyway, Lucius commanded his charges to stay put. Then, transforming into a dark-brown seagull, he flew up and over the ships.

Hovering over the decks, and the men toiling on them, he gathered the information he needed. Flying back to Lilith and Bestias, he landed behind a pile of garbage deep in the recesses of the alley. He emerged in his human guise and rejoined the other two.

"This ship in front of us—it has a cargo of grain, and will set sail tomorrow for Byzantium, taking the coastal route. We will wait until dark and board the vessel. It would be best to spend the journey in the hold of the ship. It will be dark, and the grain will attract the—vermin—that you two will need to sustain you. If it weren't for someone," here he threw a glare at Bestias, "we could just make the journey by our usual way. However, that talent has yet to be awakened in you."

Bestias glared back, a look that would have killed a mortal. Lucius ignored him.

They waited until the purple twilight had given way to black night. There was no moon, and the stars gave little light to the slaves still working on the decks.

An old man sat in the doorway of a building near where the trio was hidden. He had a blanket draped over him; just one of the myriad of homeless who littered the land like so much seaweed on a beach. As the trio ascended the gangplank of the great ship opposite him, the transient looked up at the deck. He surreptitiously touched his wrist. Another man, a sailor strolling the deck, caught the movement and nodded imperceptibly. The new passengers were noted.

Bestias was almost uncontrollable by the time they reached the hold. Once they were in its darkest depths, he fell on the first rodent he saw.

What a surprise it was to find that his own teeth grew immediately into fangs. No more did he need Lilith's help; he tore into the creature with savage need, draining its blood in seconds. He panted in his excitement, scenting out more.

Lilith watched him. She was more willing to wait patiently; with her thousands of years of experience, she knew that there would always be another victim as long as the Creator allowed the generation of his creatures to continue.

Without taking her eyes off her newest acquisition, she grabbed a passing rat, sucked it dry, and threw it onto a growing pile. Bored with him already, she was not looking forward to the centuries she knew she would have with him by her side. *Pity*.

Bestias scrabbled around the hold, until Lucius brought him up short with the bark of an order. "Stop! We have a long journey ahead of us, and a limited supply of vermin."

Bestias looked at him, confused. "There will be a boatload of men. You don't expect me to ignore such a treasure. The rats are temporary, until we get under way?"

"No, this sustenance is not temporary, and, yes, I expect you to limit your hunger to the four-footed variety of victims. After all, who will sail the ship if you consume the crew?"

Bestias threw down the rat he had just picked up. "You made me this way! Now you expect me to not act in the way I was created?"

He picked up a large, heavy clay jar and threw it against the wall in frustration and anger.

"What's happening down there?" A lone figure appeared in the doorway. The trio slipped back further into the shadows of the hold as a large, burly sailor came into view.

"I want you slaves off my ship," he ordered at the air around him. "Hiding in here to escape will not help you. I will return you to your masters, and I won't mind the reward money at all!" He walked further into the hold, casting his eyes about warily as he looked for imagined refugees.

Lucius sighed as he glanced over at Bestias. The creature was drooling, his eyes blazing, as he watched the sailor. Lucius raised an arm, swept it through the air.

At the same time, the surprised sailor was lifted from the ground, and before he could cry out, was dashed against the hull of the ship. He slid to the floor, unconscious.

Lucius turned to Bestias. "There is your supply for the journey. Make it last."

Lilith moved toward the body, but Lucius stopped her. "You find your own."

She hissed at him but stepped back, glaring at both him and Bestias, who had already pounced on the luckless crewman.

All's fair in war and hunger, then...she narrowed her eyes at her once-treasured Bestias.

Lucius made an impatient noise in his throat. He strode over and pulled Bestias up by his hair. Bestias' fangs caught in his victim's neck, pulling the man up with him. The body tore away, slumping to the floor, the throat torn beyond repair.

Bestias whimpered as he looked longingly at the man. He reached for his dinner, but was held immobile in the grip of his demonic master. "You idiot," hissed Lucius. "Did I not just tell you to have some control over yourself? Now he's dead, and totally useless to any of us."

He let Bestias go. The novice vampire looked helplessly at the inert figure, then at Lucius. He bent down, scooped up the blood welling from the torn throat, and shoved the gore into his mouth. Looking again at Lucius, he asked, "Can't you fix him?"

Lucius abruptly turned and strode away angrily. "No, I do not have that power. Only—*He*— has that privilege."

"Who? God?" It was asked in all innocence.

Lucius whirled on Bestias, drove the fullness of his power into the vampire in all its fury. "Do...NOT...mention that...Name...in my presence!" he roared.

Lilith interposed herself between the two. "Remember, he knows very little about his awakened life," she reminded Lucius. "Do not forget why he was created as well. His final use is more important than your little snit."

Lucius growled, and lightning flashing in his eyes. He turned away and replied, "He'd better learn some control, if you two are to survive this journey."

Lilith kept watch in the gangway as the other two dragged the body up to the deck and tossed it over the rail. Before they came back, however, she stole away in search of her own victim.

It was a little early to find someone on board that wouldn't be missed; killing that man was a really bad move, to her mind. Better to troll for dinner in the anonymity of the city.

She stole down the gangplank and followed a couple of sailors to a tavern. There she hid behind some detritus in an alley and waited.

Soon a lone figure lurched its way drunkenly out of the tavern, and headed unsteadily in her direction. Lilith wasn't too happy with alcohol-laden blood, but it was better than going hungry. She was about to make her move when a woman approached the drunk. Snarling in frustration, Lilith ducked back into her hiding place. She watched as the two whispered together, then smiled slowly, licking her fangs, as they made their way down her alley.

Two rather than one. Well, it was a challenge, but it would make the trip to Byzantium easier to endure. She was able to put away an immense amount of human life-fluids after so many centuries of preying on them.

Giggling, the woman—obviously a whore— came past Lilith's hiding spot first. She held the man's hand and eagerly pulled him along with her. Without a sound, Lilith leapt out as he passed. With one bite, she severed the vulnerable vein in his throat. He fell, an attempt at a scream gurgling, lost in his blood.

The girl turned, eyes wide. Her terrified gaze fell on Lilith, and she would have screamed in turn, but the she-devil lashed out with her talons and tore out the streetwalker's throat. Not a sound of struggle came from the darkened alleyway as the vampire took another victim.

Lilith sated herself on the pair. Afterwards, she wondered idly if she should do something with the bodies. Finally, she decided she'd leave them where they were. If the Hunters were to find them, what would it matter? The three of them would be gone, up the coast to Byzantium, and their pursuers would be none the wiser. After all, ships left out of this harbor many times a day—they'd have no idea which one they'd gotten on, if any.

She headed back to the ship, after wiping her gore-smeared face on the man's tunic.

While she was gone, Lucius and Bestias had returned to the hold. Bestias sat in a corner, licking his fangs. The blood-lust rose on occasion, but he knew he had to quell it in front of Lucius. He still wasn't sure what the extent of the dark demon's powers were, but he knew they far exceeded his own paltry abilities. Covering his mouth to suppress a moan of hunger, he pulled his cloak over his head and wished for the dead-sleep.

Lucius paced back and forth, his impatience growing by the minute. Where was Lilith? She knew she couldn't escape. It was rather surprising that she had been gone when he and Bestias had returned. Centuries ago, she had pulled a stunt just like this, and learned quite painfully that such an endeavor was impossible. He could easily find her if need be, but he chose to wait, letting his fury grow, so that he could make her existence that much more excruciating.

Just as he had decided to pursue her, she appeared within the hold. He was disappointed; he had been looking forward to inflicting pain on her. "Where have you been?" he demanded.

She tossed him a look and found a vacant corner. "I have needs too. At this point in time, however, I didn't want to decrease the crew size any more than it has been," she said, barely hiding direct accusation. He knew what she meant though, and made mental record of it.

"Now, I'm going to try to sleep away as much of this little sea adventure as I can." She wrapped her cloak around her, looked defiantly at Lucius, and turned towards the wall.

Bestias decided it was best to just pretend to be asleep as well, which left Lucius standing alone in the hold. He sat down on some cargo, fuming, with no one to spend his rage on. Being attached to this particular project of the Master's was taking its toll on him, but until it was fully developed, he was stuck with these two. And there was no end of this until the right one was found to complete the creation. He stared sourly at Bestias.

If it wasn't for the absolute guarantee of the success of this plan, he'd let the Hunters find and destroy both Bestias and Lilith. They definitely had the means to do so; the wood of that Cross was all that was needed, and it wouldn't be difficult to distribute all those tiny pieces worldwide. After all, he knew, the world was so much larger than the Romans of this age could even imagine...

Most of the voyage went smoothly, the sea and wind cooperating to make the journey an easy one. Once they were certain of the weather, the crew relaxed, knowing that they would make their ports of call on time. Wine was brought out, and the men toasted their good fortune every chance they got. Evenings were filled with drunken brawling and singing, as the men left their chores of the day and readied for a night's rest.

One night, Lucius watched the men, a darker shadow among the recesses on deck, as they staggered about their duties. He smirked to himself, and melted back down into the hold.

Bestias was just stirring, as Lucius had expected. Lilith had obviously had a big kill when she was gone in Tyre; she was still rolled up in her cloak, sound asleep. Lucius watched as the monster awoke, his eyes red and crazed as he felt an aching, uncontrollable hunger. His gaze fixed on Lucius, and in his frenzy he jumped up to attack him.

Lucius held him off with just a look. Bestias beheld that terrible glare and shrank back against the wall.

"I will let you hunt," Lucius growled, "if you think you can show some self-control. You may not know this, so I must warn you: there is a limit to what you can take from a man before he goes beyond death. We want no one to awaken on this ship." Actually, Lucius wanted to see just how far Bestias could go, how much he could consume—his limits, in other words. It would be useful to know what kind of soul would be needed to complete this creation. However, in this limited environment it would be too dangerous, so self-control was key.

Bestias nodded, staring at Lucius, poised to run.

The dark man stepped aside and indicated the door. Bestias flew out of it, eagerly making his way to the deck. Lucius looked at Lilith's sleeping body and followed Bestias out. She would be safe enough—no one dared come down to the hold after hearing the ghastly howls and groans Lucius made on a regular basis.

The monster had already found a victim. The man's eyes were wide with terror, his hands tearing at Bestias, his mouth open in a silent scream. Bestias grunted in inhuman pleasure as he pulled the sailor's lifeblood from his throat. The man's eyes widened when he saw Lucius, and he reached out in desperation to who he hoped was his salvation. Lucius smiled humorlessly as he watched the life go out of him.

The smile left abruptly, as Lucius noticed something terribly wrong. He knew the signs, but he hadn't expected this sort of thing to happen so early in Bestias' career.

Lucius acted quickly, putting his hand under Bestias' chin and pulling him off of his victim. Bestias whined in frustration as he fought to get back to his feast, but Lucius threw him to one side.

The sailor's eyes, so dead just a minute ago, were now blazing with an unnatural light. He sat up, growling, and looked around him. Lucius grabbed him before he could get away, and held him fast by the throat. He turned and spat his fury at Bestias. "Fool! I don't know how you did it, but you seem to have produced your first offspring."

Bestias looked at Lucius, confused. "What do you mean?" he asked.

"This...man!" Lucius shook the sailor as if he was a mere rag. "You've caused him to awaken. He is one of...you. Under other circumstances, this would be commendable, but NOT ON BOARD THIS SHIP! There are just too few mortals to feed any more than you and Lilith."

He thought for a moment. The man dangling by Lucius' grip swiped at him with unnaturally long claws and growled. Without looking at him, Lucius shifted his hold to the man's tunic in a move so swift even Bestias couldn't follow it.

"Quiet, you. I'm trying to decide your fate." The man slumped as if dead.

Lucius considered the inert body. "Hmm, I like him better already. Does what he's told. However," he sighed to himself, "the Master wants the ones we have, and I have no say in the matter." He produced a long knife, and with one blow decapitated the newly-born vampire. He threw the head and body overboard.

"Too bad." Lucius watched as the water's depths swallowed up yet another seaman, its surface betraying nothing. He grabbed Bestias and dragged him back down into the hold. Lilith remained asleep; Lucius knew, however, that she would soon arise, voracious. He shook his head. This trip couldn't end soon enough.

He shoved Bestias back into his corner. "Go back to sleep," he ordered his monster.

Bestias glared at him, and sat straight up with his arms around his knees, defiant. "I think not. I am still hungry. There must be more vermin around here." In a barely-hissed whisper, he added, "...besides you."

"I heard that," Lucius growled. "Rest assured you are safe for now, since I do not need Lilith waking up before it is absolutely necessary. So I will let it pass...this time."

Bestias stared into the darkness, waiting for the glowing shapes that meant the return of the rats. With as much grain as this ship was carrying, there had to be hundreds of the creatures feeding on it.

Lilith woke and, without a word, stood up and shuffled out of the hold. A minute later there was a strangled cry from above, and a splash soon afterward, as Lilith disposed of the victim. She soon reappeared, returned to her corner, and went back to sleep.

The journey, which had started out so well, was now experiencing difficulties. The seasonal wind from the north was now pushing against the ship, and all hands were required to man the oars. Still, the ship barely crept up the coast, making their ports a little later each stop.

And after the ship left port, bodies were found in alleyways drained of blood, terror in their dead eyes.

After a long battle against the elements, the ship finally turned up the channel that led to Byzantium. Unfortunately for the crew, the undead cargo they unwittingly carried with them was relentlessly hungry. Even though Lilith and Bestias were careful with the amount they took from their victims, and Lucius caused the crew to forget the attacks, the men were getting progressively weaker.

Once the south wind won dominance in the skies again, the ship moved faster and more easily. Because of the attacks on them, however, the crew could barely get enough physical energy to control the vessel, and they were almost totally at the mercy of the tides and currents. As the channel grew narrower, they found themselves grating across hidden shoals and rocks. Towards sunset, the crew had to struggle to keep the ship in the center of the waterway.

Two men were bringing in their fishing boats down-shore from their village when one of them happened to look towards the sunset. He shouted in surprise and alarm, pointing.

A Roman merchant ship was heading directly toward the rocky coast west of their beachhead. The two men looked on helplessly as the vessel crashed into the sharp crags and boulders.

One of the men ran to the village to get help, while the other started toward the ship. Then he stopped, squinting into the new dusk.

What was that—some movement above the sea, among the rocks? That wasn't possible—those rocks were too sharp and steep for anyone to navigate. Yet there seemed to be movement. Dark shapes moving—floating?—over the surface. He shook his head. This is what happened when he spent too much time on the water. Seeing things...

Looking again, he saw nothing out of the ordinary.

What he didn't see was the dark head bobbing on the water between ship and shore. As the villagers came out and swarmed down the beach, the figure in the water waited. Once the crowd had gone by, he swam toward the shore and pulled himself from the water. He looked at the remains of the battered ship, knowing that the entire crew was dead—and not because of the shipwreck—and glanced up into the rocks above the wreck.

Touching the livid scar on his wrist, he nodded grimly to himself, and made his way toward the village.

CHAPTER 20

The sights and sounds of the busy tavern unnerved Bestias. In his mortal days, an enclosed room busy with people had made him uneasy; with his heightened perception, it was near maddening.

Even with the majority of the men and older boys down the shore attending to the foundered ship, the room was still crowded. Old men, wanton women, and those unable to make the trip towards the night's excitement filled the small space. Even some of the wives and children were starting to arrive. Everyone knew what had happened. Now they awaited further details from the rescue party.

Bestias stood nervously outside the door as the villagers came and went. The smoke that filled the room burned his eyes, and made it difficult to make out the presence or absence of any perceived danger. He was having an extremely hard time controlling his hunger; the smell of sweat and filth could not mask the throb and flow, the rich odor, of living human blood. It was all he could do to not fall on the nearest ones, regardless of the danger.

A hard hand gripped his shoulder. Lucius, behind him, pushed Bestias toward the door. "Go. Find out what we need to know." He peered closely at Bestias and saw mad, red eyes, the points of fangs just showing, the fingers twitching as the talons tried to emerge.

"Never mind. I'll go first." Lucius turned to Lilith. "Keep him under control."

Lilith grabbed Bestias' elbow, allowing one talon to emerge enough to cause him slight pain. Bestias winced, knowing that there was more where that came from, and obeyed docilely. She hissed in his ear, "It's hard for me too, but we will have all we want in due time."

The three entered the tavern and melted into a dark corner where they could be out of the way but still hear what was going on.

"Why, exactly, are we here? Shouldn't we be looking for refuge, for—sustenance—away from these crowds?" Lilith whispered to Lucius.

"Precisely why we're here. Soon enough we will get the information we need."

There was a commotion at the doorway, as a teenaged girl poked her head in and shouted, "They're back!"

Everyone ran toward the door, but they rolled back like an ocean wave as a new crowd pressed its way in. Questions were shouted, voices were raised, a cacophony of noise—until people started to notice the looks on the rescuers' faces.

To a man, they were pale, shocked, almost speechless.

The clamor died down immediately. A small dog whimpered and crawled under a table, and two wolf-like hounds howled and had to be dragged outside.

Drinks were placed in the rescuers' hands as fast as they could be poured. They were downed just as rapidly.

Everyone waited breathlessly. Finally, one of those who had gone down to the beach stepped forward. He wiped a filthy sleeve across his mouth, looked around, and shook his head. It was as if he couldn't bring himself to say what they had seen.

"Fahri, what is it? What did you see? Were there survivors?" An old man grasped the younger one's arm.

Fahri looked at the questioner without really seeing him. The others behind him were just as dead-eyed. "No survivors." He swallowed hard, sat down at a table, and gripped it until his knuckles showed white. "But it was more than that. There was something wrong on board. The crew didn't die from the crash. They were...pale, their eyes, every one of them, open, frightened. Their throats...oh, God, how I wish we hadn't gone on board. Their throats were gashed as if by some huge beast! Blood on the deck of the ship..."

The room burst into one big sound—questions, accusations, predictions, assumptions. Fahri looked into the depths of his cup, drained it, and nodded thanks as it was filled again.

Two men near the three lurkers speculated between each other, oblivious to the unholy trio listening to their conversation.

"Wonder what they were carrying? You know how Rome likes wild beasts in its games."

"Don't know. Doesn't matter, though, does it? The Romans will notice when the ship doesn't show up in a reasonable amount of time, and will come looking for it."

"Best we stay away from it. The last thing we need is for those bastards to come set up their posts here in our town. Shouldn't give them a reason to."

"But shouldn't we do something for the crew?"

"Not in my opinion. What if they've been cursed? If we do something, it might spread to us, and then..."

He stopped suddenly as a colorful newcomer staggered into the tavern. The man was dark-skinned, obviously drunk, and his clothes made everyone else's drab by comparison. Swaying in the doorway, he smiled benignly on the crowd and belched.

"You!" roared the tavern-keeper. "Get out! I told you before that you mountain-dwellers were not allowed in here."

The man ignored him and swung his hand around, begging. Two tavern patrons grabbed the unwanted fellow and wrestled him back out and into the street.

"Beggars. Ought to just get rid of them," someone said.

The conversation once again turned to the excitement of the night. Lilith and Bestias were getting bored and restless, but Lucius stood calmly in the dark, observing the ebb and flow of humanity.

Suddenly he stiffened, alarm and fury in his voice. "We must go! Now!"

The other two were only too happy to obey this time. They sprang away from the corner, not caring why Lucius suddenly gave the order. Once they were outside, though, Lucius still seemed like a cornered animal.

"There's someone in there. I don't know who it is, but someone powerful is in that room. Or he has something, a threat to us somehow," he gasped.

Lilith looked at him in wonder. She had never seen her master show such weakness before. She put this information away in her memory, ready to exploit it when she needed it. Outwardly, though, she did her best to look concerned. "Who do you think it was?"

"I've no idea!" he snarled.

A sound from Bestias drew their attention. He was staring down the narrow dirt lane between the buildings. They followed his gaze.

The mountain-dweller was reeling off into the distance. At once, Lilith understood Bestias' reason for his intense interest. "Ohhh..." she nearly swooned. "Such rich blood! Such life! I must have him."

Bestias hissed at her, and she made as if to attack him. Lucius immediately stepped between them, menace in his voice. "Stop, both of you. I can create the illusion of invisibility only if you two are quiet. Neither of you will have that mortal, you may as well know that right now."

Disappointment on Bestias' face, shock and rage on Lilith's. "What?"

Lucius stopped her with a glance. "We must follow him, find his people, and then see where they go. If they dwell in the mountains, it would mean their population is few and far between. We would not be noticed as much, and can pick and choose who we wish to join our little band. Until then, hunt the lesser animals."

The three of them continued to argue in hushed tones as they followed the drunk out of town.

In the tavern, a man sat alone in a corner and watched them go. He flipped a small piece of wood between his fingers and considered his next move.

Bestias was starting to settle into his new reality, and decided that it wasn't so bad. He could move swiftly, not get tired, and best of all, he seemed to no longer have a conscience. That particular mortal burden had disappeared once he had fully awakened, and he didn't miss it a bit.

The undead trio flitted from shadow to shadow, blending in with the night. They followed the mountain-dweller, who to Bestias' eyes looked like a rich crimson blob of light. He had to look away and rely on the other two to keep an eye on their prey; he wanted that blood so badly that he couldn't trust himself to look at the man for long.

The lone traveler staggered into a camp deep in the woods. There were several other individuals, men and women, sitting at a fire. Immediately an argument broke out between the newcomer and some of the men. Bestias caught "money" mentioned several times, and suddenly realized that he had no trouble understanding these peoples' language, even though he'd never heard it before. He wondered vaguely if he could speak it as well. He tried a couple of words he'd heard, whispering them to himself. "'Bani'—money. 'Beat'—drunk. 'Cârciumâ'—tavern..."

"Quiet!" Lilith hissed at him.

Bestias looked sullenly at her, hunched down into himself, and stared at the arguing figures at the campsite. She never let him have any fun...

Suddenly there was a low rumbling sound beside him. Lilith was purring; Bestias knew that sound only too well. It meant that she had her eye on one of the men.

Lucius sighed. "No."

"Oh, come on," Lilith pleaded in hushed tones. "He wouldn't take up much room, and besides, I'm getting hungry."

"For what? Mortal blood or just another conquest?"

Bestias flinched.

'Conquest'? Was that all he was? A voice whispered in his head. "Yes." It was Cain, still waiting for his turn at full existence.

Bestias shook his head. *Go away!!* he mentally screamed at Cain.

Lucius peered at the group. It had increased by two, and he could readily see which one had interested Lilith.

"The man with the curly dark hair? Red shirt, no beard?"

"Yes," Lilith breathed.

"What sets him apart?"

Lilith looked at Lucius in surprise. "Don't you see that delicious, virile red haze that envelops him? Plus, he's terribly handsome too. He'd make a terrific trophy."

Lucius, puzzled, looked again. "I have never seen a glow around any mortal. But then again, I do not have the needs you have.

A moment's scrutiny later: "Wait." He held up his hand. "Do you see? Right at the very core of his being. It's a vacant spot—not very big, but it's perfect for habitation! See how kind he is to his fellows; but he has a penchant for violence, which often negates any good he has done. That is the sort of material that is best for the awakening."

They watched as the man in question arbitrated the argument, clapped the men good-naturedly on their shoulders, and, smiling, returned to his place by the fire.

Bestias' eyes followed him, and he found his gaze riveted to the young woman who sat beside him at the fire. Her glow was a royal crimson, a red so shiningly beautiful, not to mention tantalizing, that he had to curl his fingers into the tree he was hiding behind to keep from rushing out at her.

"So you've seen her." Lucius laughed low in his throat. "Wondered how long it would take." He cupped his chin in his hand, thinking. Lilith and Bestias watched him hopefully. "Hmm. Well, we don't know where we'll end up, and we may get lost..."

The other two quivered in mounting excitement.

"It would be better if you two had a couple of...cows...so we wouldn't have to spend all night hunting..."

It was all Lilith could do not to jump up and down. She had played this game before, many thousands of times over the eons.

"However..."

A cold wind seemed to blow across the vampires' minds. Their disappointment was palpable in the midnight air. Lilith, especially, felt her hopes plummeting.

Lucius whispered to her, "You see, you don't know me all that well. Keep that in mind when you make your little plans."

Lilith's memory returned to Lucius' fright at the tavern. She shuddered, realizing that he had known what she had been thinking.

Lucius continued, "We mustn't make a move yet. We are too close to the village, and they are still sending out the news about the ship. These people will be on their guard, and we need them to show us how to get somewhere that is not heavily populated."

"Why don't we just go up to them and introduce ourselves? Say we're travelers, and ask to join them?" Bestias asked innocently.

Lilith rolled her eyes and snorted derisively. She was about to retort when Lucius hushed her with a look.

"Bestias. Think about what you just said," Lucius replied. "First of all, we can hardly join their caravan when *they* travel during the day, and you and Lilith are, for all intents and purposes, *dead* while the sun is up. Second, if we show up, their first thought would be that we came from that ship, and so might possibly be a part of whatever cursed the crew. True, but they don't need to know that. Do you see the problem?"

Bestias slowly nodded. "Then how are we to follow them?" he asked Lucius. "By the time the sun sets tomorrow, they will have probably gone far from here."

"You have a point. Hmmm..." Lucius gave this some thought. "Well, we'll just worry about that tomorrow. Perhaps we can follow someone else."

Lilith and Bestias looked toward the campsite, devastated. Lucius rubbed his hands together briskly, purposely oblivious to their distress. "Now," he said cheerfully, "let's find you two someone to feed on, shall we?"

They made their way back silently through the undergrowth, the leaves and twigs parting before them as if afraid of being touched by their evil. The only sound came from the two vampires, who were whispering bitter accusations at each other.

"Probably your fault. You just had to be so obvious about that man."

"You're just jealous," Lilith sniffed.

"And why shouldn't I be? Not a half-year ago you were drooling over me in the same way."

"That was when you were mortal. It was your blood I wanted, although the physical bit would have been a nice distraction."

"That's all I was to you? A conquest?"

"Quiet, both of you," hissed Lucius. "I've heard quite enough. You'll scare the wildlife away if you keep this bickering up.

"Look! There's your dinner." He pointed to a huge stag that was standing in front of a grove of trees, grazing in a patch of moonlit vegetation. It hadn't heard the three approaching; Lucius had to use all of his powers of illusion to keep it from being frightened away by his noisy charges.

Bestias started towards the deer, but was pushed out of the way by Lilith. He ran up and pulled at her, making her stumble, and they started tearing and raking at each other. The deer's head went up and, startled, it bounded off through the trees.

"You idiots! There goes your sustenance!" Lucius roared, grabbing both of them by their arms. A purple bolt of lightning shot through both vampires, and they screamed in agony as the energy charged into them.

Lucius released them with a push that caused them to sprawl onto the ground. Bestias was surprised to see a scrape on his arm, surprised even more to see that it was bleeding. Lilith saw it at the same time. She leapt at Bestias, her blazing red eyes riveted on the stream that oozed from his arm. Bestias snarled and swiped at her, and she screeched as she dodged his claws. He scrabbled away backwards, angrily sucking on the wound.

"Mine! Get your own!" he ordered.

Lucius swore. If he could ever have a chance to lose these two, he'd take it and be done with them. "Stop it, both of you!" he shouted, sparks shooting from his eyes.

He stood and watched them as they sat, stonily facing away from each other. The silence was deafening. After a while, Lucius cleared his throat. "Done with your tantrums?" he asked.

Both of them hesitated, then nodded grudgingly.

"You two will be spending a very long time with each other. Oh, pardon...you *three*. I forgot."

Bestias growled, two voices emanating from his throat. Lucius ignored it. "Therefore, it would be beneficial to all of you to rely on each other for help, instead of complaining and fighting at the least impulse.

"Therefore, you will try this..."

He merely looked at them, and suddenly Bestias could feel his body change. His arms grew, the claws changing into wolf-like paws. His nose elongated, and his vision changed. Where once there were colors, now were shades of grey and blue. The loss of color vision was replaced by an entire universe of new odors, and as he padded around in his new body, his every step stirred up more.

"Hunting as wolves will make the hunt go faster and will teach you two a lesson in cooperation," Lucius said.

Lilith had become a wolf as well, and the two of them readily picked up the scent of the deer at the same time. They both started running, tongues lolling as they loped swiftly over the ground.

It didn't take them long to find not only the stag, but a couple of does as well. Furtively, they circled through the underbrush, waited, then leapt out at their victims.

It was so easy! Almost as if it had been planned. They tore into the throats of the two deer, and lapped at the blood flowing from the wounded flesh.

The excitement at this turn of events died quickly, however. It was far too slow this way.

Again, something new! All Bestias had to do was to think of his human form, and he was himself again. Lilith had returned to herself too. She was stained head to foot, her beautiful alabaster skin drenched with the animal's blood.

They drank greedily, practically rolling in the gore.

Suddenly a thought dawned on Bestias. Could it be? It seemed as if they were completely alone; Lucius was nowhere in sight. He got up slowly, peering into the shadows.

"What?" Lilith asked, looking up from her kill.

"Lucius didn't follow us. We're…"

"Alone? Hardly. He always finds who he's looking for."

"Well, he won't find me. I'm getting away while I can. You can stay with that creature, or demon, or whatever, but I'm setting out on my own."

"Suit yourself," Lilith mumbled, her face back down in the deer.

"Really?" Bestias could hardly believe his ears. He turned and walked, first slowly, then much faster. Soon he was crashing through the forest, getting further and further from his oppressive companions.

Back at the clearing, Lucius appeared by Lilith, who was now finishing off Bestias' deer. "So he's gone."

She nodded, slurping with gusto.

Lucius stared off into the direction Bestias had taken. "Well, let's go get him."

Lilith looked up, gore running from her mouth. "Must we? I miss the times when it was just the two of us. He's annoying."

"We have a mission. There is no choice in the matter."

"Oh, if we must, we must." She sighed and got up. "Let's go."

The two melted off into the shadows, following Bestias' unmistakable scent.

Bestias climbed to the top of a wall of boulders, intent on a small leopard. It lay with its back to him, its tail flicking as it watched something in the glen below. Instead of changing to wolf form, which Bestias had been practicing ever since he felt he'd gotten safely away, he was in his human form. Climbing rock walls was far easier with fingers than with canine paws.

The leopard never knew what hit it. Bestias had his fangs in its throat before it could make a sound. As he fed, his gaze wandered down to what the leopard had been so intent on.

What he saw made him freeze in place, dropping the cat. He stared in disbelief.

It was the girl from the campsite!

She was bathing in a quiet, moonlit pool, swimming slowly, luxuriating in the isolation of this place. Bestias smiled to himself. How gallant of him to have saved her from this savage cat—just so that he could have her for himself. Ah, the irony.

He crept stealthily down the rock face and hid in the darkness on the shore. Still as the boulders that surrounded the pool, he watched her, letting his hunger grow.

Oh, sweet beauty of youth! He admired her form as she pulled herself out of the water and sat on a rock close to shore, her back to him. She ran her fingers through her hair, singing softly to herself. There was a time, Bestias recalled, when his desire would have been of a far more physical nature, and by now they'd be rolling on the forest floor, be she willing or not.

Now all that consumed him was bloodlust. He let it rise in him until it was unbearable, and then he made his move.

He slid silently into the water, just another hiss and slap of water on shore. Hesitating, he watched for any sign that she had heard him. She continued to hum and play with her hair, not suspecting a thing.

Closer he floated, not rippling the water any more than he had to. It took all of his willpower to keep his breathing even. He came up behind her and put his claws on the wet, mossy rock. Slowly and silently, he rose up out of the water. Her shoulders were white in the moonlight, and the thought of them running red with her blood made him almost moan with desire.

Suddenly she spun around, saw him, and sucked in her breath to scream. Before she could, he had her by that glorious hair. He pulled her off the rock and held her underwater. Her eyes flew open in horror, and she twisted and fought him, fought for breath. Her scream came out in a large bubble of air, and as she took in lungfuls of water, she slowly stopped fighting and went limp.

Quickly, Bestias pulled her out and laid her across the rock, exposing her neck. Now for that feast he so richly deserved...

He plunged into her throat, feeling both the pulse and the warm fluid spurting into his mouth.

A crash and a shout from the opposite side of the pond made him look up, his eyes blazing and his face and neck running red with her blood. A man stood, stricken with terror, as he beheld the nightmare before him.

"Amalie!" he cried, and lunged toward them, heedless of the danger.

A screech, and Lilith was on the man, her eyes black, her mouth in a wide-open grimace. Her victim had no time to defend himself as she lay across him, her head at his throat.

Bestias went back to his own feast.

A hand touched him and he shook it off. The next moment, he found himself pulled up and away from the girl, dangling in the air at the end of Lucius' arm.

"Enough! These two are not to be used up all in one night."

He let Bestias down and took up the woman in his arms. As he carried her to shore, he reprimanded Bestias, "And you—trying to run away from us. I'm going to let you off lightly this time," here he sent a wave of energy into

Bestias that made him double over, howling in agony, "but let this be a lesson to you. I always know where you are. And now that the very thing I told you NOT to do has been done, and you have taken her, we shall have to bend this situation to our advantage. Fortunately for you both, this solves the problem of how we will get to our destination. Now—let's get her dressed, and when these two wake up they will be our eyes and ears for the journey."

Lilith joined them where the girl had discarded her clothes. She had the man by the hair, and was dragging him as effortlessly as a child would a toy.

"Bring them with us," Lucius ordered. "There is a cave a short distance from here. Lilith!" He had turned and saw her still dragging her victim.

Motioning to Bestias, he said, "Carry that one so he has some skin left on him by the time we get there." He looked reprovingly at Lilith.

"All those open sores would have been a pleasant diversion," she drawled.

Lucius ignored her and set out, carrying the girl. "'Amalie'," he muttered to himself. "Means 'work', I believe. Hmph, can't be any harder work than what Lilith's caused me."

Bestias followed behind, carrying the man. Lilith brought up the rear, catching small, winged night creatures and snacking on the treasure in their veins as she went.

Once they were in the darkest recesses of the cave, Lilith found a niche in a wall and went into death. Bestias followed suit, after laying the man next to Amalie.

Lucius stood near the entrance and watched the night slowly turn to day.

The sound of frightened whispers drew Lucius out of the reverie he usually escaped to during the interminably boring hours of daylight. He listened closely.

"Bogdan? Where are we?"

So that was his name. Lucius chuckled. Bogdan. Meant "God-given".

Well, thanks, Creator. I didn't expect such a nice gift; and here I didn't get you anything...

Bogdan spoke. "I don't know. Look! It's daylight—we have to get back before everyone starts to miss us. Here, I'll help you up."

There was some scuffling, a thud, and then sounds of fear and disbelief.

"Amalie, I am so weak. Are you okay? I didn't mean to let you fall."

"I...I'm weak too. I don't understand it."

"Let's just catch our breath and try again. Maybe it's the close air in this cave that's doing it. See the light over there? It must be the entrance."

"I hope you're right. Oh, the family is going to be so angry with us."

"They'll be especially angry because they weren't able to start back towards home in the early morning. That shipwreck...you know that the villagers are saying we caused it."

"What? Why?"

"Grandfather says that they think it happened at the same time he had come into town, and they think he cursed it."

"Well, that's stupid."

"Still..."

"I'm getting up...ooh, I'm sitting down."

"Here, stand up again," Bogdan encouraged her. "We'll lean on each other to get back. I'm sure we'll be fine once we have some of Grandmother's herbs."

"Bogdan, do you remember anything from last night?" Amalie's voice was perplexed.

After a moment, Bogdan responded, "No, I don't. It's as if nothing happened between when we left to get some privacy last night and when we woke up. It's strange. I don't like it."

"Bogdan, I'm scared."

"The sooner we're gone from here the better. Let's try again."

Their labored grunts and footsteps became louder as they drew near the entrance. Lucius made his presence known once they had rounded the curve into full sunlight. He smiled to himself as they shrank back from the light.

"Good morning, children."

Bogdan peered at Lucius from under the hand he'd put up to shield his eyes from the glare. Pain danced in his eyes, but he dared not back down from this stranger, for both his and Amalie's sakes. "Who are you? Did you bring us here?" His voice became angry as this sudden insight changed fear and trepidation into rage. He lunged at Lucius, but tripped in his weakness, bringing both himself and Amalie down.

Lucius clucked sympathetically. "Here, let me help you up."

The instant he touched them, both mortals went stiff. The light in their eyes died, as did all animation in their faces.

"Now that I have your attention..." Lucius crooned. He paced back and forth in front of his inert audience, his fingers tented before his chest. "You now have a new life. It will be of far more use to you than your old one. We have need of your protection and guidance to where your clan is going.

"What you will do is this: you will return to your people, and say nothing about our...agreement. In fact, you will not remember me, or having had this conversation. You will pack your things and return here once the sun has gone down. No one must see you leave. The next day your family will see that your things are gone, and will believe that the two of you have set off alone to make your own way in the world.

"You will return here, to do our bidding and to show us how to get into those mountains you call home. In time, you will be amply rewarded. If you disobey, the results will be...rather unpleasant. Now go."

Bogdan and Amalie woke out of their trance to find themselves alone. They looked at each other, and got up slowly. Surprised at how much stronger they felt, they fell into each other's arms and laughed in relief.

"Guess we just needed to sleep a little longer. Still, let's get some distance between us and this place." Amalie linked her arm in Bodgan's and they set off to find the camp.

Bogdan stopped after a few steps, and looked back. "Still, I wonder..."

"Don't," Amalie begged him. "I don't want to remember now."

That night, at midnight, Amalie and Bogdan were back. How and why it happened, they could not say.

Bewildered, the couple took in the cave entrance and the moonlight washing the path before it. They clutched their satchels in front of them.

"Bogdan, why are we here again?"

"I...I don't know," he whispered.

They froze at a sound from the depths of the cave. Two figures emerged: a woman, raven-haired, seeming to glow in the darkness; and a man, dark-skinned, with curly brown hair. What struck terror into the two young people, however, was the look in their eyes. It was the look of sheer eviland something else...

That was all Amalie and Bogdan had time to ponder. Lilith and Bestias flew at their victims, sating themselves on the crimson stream that flowed out of their veins.

The next night, after Amalie and Bogdan had recovered, and after Lilith and Bestias had had another small feed, they all set forth. The two young mortals led the way, half-dead but feeling no weakness, no fear, nothing but a sense of servile purpose. Bestias, Lilith, and Lucius followed, the two vampires occasionally shifting to their wolf-state to hunt.

Slowly they made their way northwest, eventually stopping and taking up residence in what would eventually become known as the Carpathian Mountains.

PART III – VLAD TEPES

CHAPTER 21

The winter wind moaned through the trees, and sent the snow-filled clouds racing across the sky. As night drew on, the shadows deepened and darkened, almost totally obscuring the lone, still figure sprawled on the deserted, muddy highway.

He had not been there for long; fresh hoof prints attested to that fact. Indeed, less than a half-hour before, he had been riding quickly back to his castle with a retinue of his most trusted guards. They had been out on patrol, looking for enemy spies. There had been rumors of infiltration in the towns between Bucharest and Wallachia, and he and his men had gone to see if they were true. When no useful information could be wrested from the town's inhabitants, he had ordered them killed.

Stupid peasants, Vlad Tepes thought as he rode through the dying population, paying little attention to their cries for mercy. *They shouldn't be allowed to breed.*

When the storm clouds had blown together late in the afternoon, and the snow had started to come down thick as wool, he had decided they should return to this game on another day. He tired of seeing his men so filthy with all that peasant gore on their fine uniforms.

Riding home, they had slipped into this copse just as the storm started to abate. Swords drawn and eyes alert, all had kept watch for any signs of encroaching life, be it human or animal. Wolves were known to be quite clever at hunting down men, and his soldiers had positively reeked with that sweet, metallic blood smell he'd grown to love.

Both wolves and bears were drawn to it, and that was something he wanted to avoid. Bears weren't so much of a problem; in fact, they tasted delicious. Those wolves, though. A real menace! If he didn't have his barbarian enemies to keep from his borders, he'd hunt down every last one of them and use their hides as rugs throughout his castle.

Suddenly a lone figure had come charging at them from the direction of Wallachia, his horse steaming and gasping under him. The party had peered at him as he drew nearer, unable to get a really good look in the dimming light. As he approached, a collective sigh of relief went up from the men; they had been able to make out that he wore the uniform of the Inner Guard.

It must be an urgent message, Vlad had thought. Was the enemy attacking his city while they had been away? He had held up his hand to stay the others from advancing, stopped his own horse, and had let the messenger come. "What news?" he had exclaimed loudly, so as to be heard by the approaching rider.

His answer had been a sword in his chest. He had looked down at it in surprise, then at his men, as he slid off his mount and down onto the road.

Eyesight dimming, he still had had enough wits to notice that not a single man pursued his attacker. They had merely turned away and kept on their path back to Wallachia. A couple of men had spat on him as they passed.

Now he lay alone, waiting for death, feeling the occasional snowflake land on him. He wondered if he would be covered in white by morning. The cold felt distant, as did the sounds of the night creatures in the darkness beneath the trees. He hoped one or two would come out and finish him off. If it was time to go to the flames, then let it happen, and quickly. He had a few things he'd like to say to The Old Buzzard, and would be glad to be out of this wet weather.

He closed his eyes for a moment, feeling the life oozing out of him from where the sword was still embedded. Odd—no pain. He wished for it. He'd never really felt alive any time in his life, and wished that, just once, he would be able to feel enough to care about something.

Without knowing how, he suddenly realized that he was not alone. Were his ears going? He hadn't heard anyone approach, but he was certain someone was standing over him. Making a tremendous effort, he opened his eyes—and was surprised to see, not one, but three figures looking down at him.

Peasants? Not with those clothes. Gypsies? Maybe, but they weren't stripping him bare for his valuables. Not yet, anyway. There was one who wore a black winter coat with a hood that hid his face. The darkness inside that hood covering was blacker than the most midnight of nightmare shadows. It seemed there was no limit to it; that if he had the energy, he could look at that "face" and see all the way into Hell itself. He wished he could try.

And the other two. They were dressed somewhat more colorfully and expensively, but looked like they'd dressed without much thought as to the current fashions. Even so, they seemed graceful, ageless somehow.

The woman...oh how beautiful! Hair dark and glossy in the pale light, black—black!—eyes, soft red lips...

...that parted in a very bewitching smile. Ah, if he could get up, she would be his.

She laughed, a short little laugh that wasn't quite a girlish giggle.

The man beside her was glaring at her. *Hmmm, jealous.* If they were a couple, he'd hack off the man's head and carry her away, where she would join the rest of his mistresses until he got tired of her. Then—head on a pike. Nothing made him feel more powerful than when he saw them die, most screaming, all horrified. And those last grimaces remained, in frozen death masks. He would often ride by the line of poles, admiring his handiwork. Never two the same.

The woman's jealous companion turned his scowl toward the dying man, who wondered vaguely if hallucinations were part of the death voyage. For this one's face kept changing—the bone structure went from fine to thick, the nose pointed and then flattened out. Even the eyes seemed to change, but it was getting too dark to tell for sure.

His thoughts were interrupted by a voice that sounded like a thousand muted funeral bells. It was coming from the hooded figure.

"Well, well, Vlad Tepes. I've waited a long time for this moment."

Tepes blinked. This man knew his true name? Most knew him as Dracul, the surname of his father and his father before him. He groaned and shifted, and a sharp pain ran through him. *Ah, pain at last...*

Tepes glared at the strangers and said through gritted teeth, "So you know who I am, eh? Well, then be good enough to help me up."

The hooded one laughed. "None of us here are 'good', Tepes. You know that." He started pacing slowly, in an attitude of deep thought. "But," he said, stopping and holding up a bony finger, "I think I know of a way to 'help' you that would be beneficial to all of us."

Tepes sighed in exasperation, wincing at the pain. He hated guessing games, and he could see through this man's schemes so easily. "Go ahead. Take my castle and everything in it. I'll sign a piece of paper stating your ownership. Then finish the job my so-called 'trusted' comrades started." He indicated the sword hilt.

"Oh, yes, that. It must be very—inconvenient—to you about now. What do you say we remove it?" The dark stranger strode over swiftly, put a boot on Vlad's chest, and pulled the sword out in one fluid movement. The blood gushed forth anew.

Vlad screamed in agony. Then, through his pain, he saw something that froze him immobile in terror, stopping his howls.

The man and woman were advancing on him. Their eyes glowed red and their open maws had the sharpest teeth he had ever seen, even sharper than a wolf's. A cold realization hit him, the terror of it freezing the very marrow in his bones.

Vampires! The talk all over the country, the speculation, all true! Those men who had come to his city...they hadn't been lying! He'd ordered their bodies to be put on pikes...this time he may have acted a little prematurely. Tepes closed his eyes, trembling and gasping in fear, unable to do anything but wait for the demons to finish him off...

"Stop, you two!" commanded the dark one. Tepes' eyes flew open again, and he watched as the vampires hissed and glared at their leader, backing away. The longing in their eyes as the red stream coursed from the wound was almost amusing to the dying man.

The dark one was livid. "Do I have to tie you to a tree? I don't know why you can't control yourselves."

Then he pointed a finger at Vlad's chest. Cold blue lightning shot from his fingertip, burning and cauterizing the sword's damage. Vlad couldn't believe his eyes. He looked from himself to his benefactor, his mouth gaping wordlessly.

Finally he found his voice. "I'm...I'm healed? You, sir, are a great wizard. Might I know your name? When we get back to Wallachia, I will make you my closest confidante. We will rid my castle of those treacherous fools. But those," he looked over at the two would-be attackers, "they would have to be destroyed. They are an abomination, a..."

"Enough!" roared the dark one. Then, a little more quietly, "Since you asked, my name is Lucius. The woman is Lilith, and the man is Bes—no, we changed it, didn't we—His name is Ivan."

Lilith and Ivan were scenting the air, which reeked of burnt flesh. Their mouths were open, and they were giddy with the smell. Vlad turned his head away in disgust.

"Now, my proposition..." Lucius began.

Tepes tried to sit up, but fell back in surprised pain. "I'm not healed? I can tell; the wound is only healed over the surface. Why just seal it up? Can't you do more than that?"

Lucius glared at Tepes, a look that could have set the wounded Count on fire if the demon so chose. Tepes actually felt the heat coming from that dark space within the hood. Terrified, he shrank back into silence.

"I do not have that power. It was taken away from me long ago," he growled. "I stopped the hemorrhage to keep those two from destroying you—for now.

"Now listen, and do not interrupt. My patience has grown shorter over time. First, a question: How would you like to live forever? No pain, no tiredness. No death, at least in mortal terms. Would you like that?"

Tepes looked over at the two undead creatures again, and he understood completely what Lucius was implying. His eyes widened in horror. "What? No! Not like that. Just let me die, and I will go and see the Old Man, and let it be my eternity."

"Ah, Vlad, you do not know what you're asking. I've been there, and it's nothing like you are imagining. I'll tell you a little secret," he whispered, bending towards the frightened mortal. "None of us ever want to be there."

The hood had come close enough to Vlad's face to let him glimpse inside.

One quick look was more than enough. He tried to back away from Lucius, heedless of the pain, but had no energy for it. Gasping and in a cold sweat, he lay staring at Lucius in sheer terror. "You're...you're...!"

Lucius nodded once.

"Wh...why me? Go away! Let me die here alone!"

"Oh, no, my boy. We can't allow that."

"Why?" Vlad managed to croak out.

"Oh, we've been following your career for years now. I must admit, your actions make some of the lesser demons look weak in comparison. My compliments, sir." Lucius bowed mockingly.

"Now, back to my question. We think you would make a perfect addition to our little family. In fact," here he pointed a finger to Lilith and Ivan, and flicked it in a silent command, "we insist on it."

That last was said in a growl so hideous that even the vampires hesitated. Lucius looked up at them, and they came forward again.

Vlad's heart stopped in horror. He couldn't breathe, couldn't move, as, leering, they knelt over him. The last thing Vlad Tepes knew in this life was the pain of needle-sharp teeth in his neck and sword wound, and the dull ache and pressure of his veins as they collapsed from swift loss of blood.

The dead Count's soul floated above his inert form as the undead killers drained it of its life fluid. Suddenly, Lilith and Ivan fell back with a cry of surprise, and Vlad could see why.

Around his body, erupting like black flumes from the ground, were several dark shapes. Some looked like spiked balls, with dark lightning flashing outward from their centers. There were also shapeless black shadows that accompanied them. They rose toward Vlad's hovering soul, reaching for him, wanting to drag him to his eternal damnation. He was all too willing to go with them, and was about to do just that, when—

"Stop!" commanded Lucius. "He belongs to us." The hellhounds retreated, hesitated for a moment, and returned to their abode.

Lucius looked up at Vlad's shade. "Ivan." Then he nodded toward the spirit hanging in mid-air. "Take him."

Ivan looked up, then at Lucius. "No, I think two of us in here is quite enough."

"Do as you're told!"

"You don't own me!" bellowed Ivan.

"I do, and the Dark One does through me. When will you admit it?"

Vlad's ghost was trying to get away, but since he knew Heaven wouldn't take him and Hell was denied, he wasn't able to go anywhere.

Lilith rolled her eyes, disgusted with all of them. Then she opened her mouth, fixing Vlad's ghost with a stare that would have killed him, had he not already been dead. He struggled, feeling his essence being drawn in, but for all his fighting soon disappeared within her.

Then she yanked Ivan around from the argument he was having with Lucius, forced his mouth open with hers, and deposited Vlad's soul into the body that housed Cain and Judas.

The body staggered back, and, once again there was internal combat as the three souls fought each other.

Lilith glared at Lucius, then at whatever this creature would turn out to be this time.

"At least someone did something right," was all the thanks she would get from her master.

She nudged the Count's body with her foot. "Couldn't we use this body? I'm so tired of looking at that one," she complained, jerking her thumb toward the crowded, embattled figure writhing on the ground.

"Perhaps. Let me...wait!" Lucius listened. "Someone's coming."

He disappeared in a flash. Lilith was about to do likewise when she remembered their "beast". She threw her hands up in frustration, seized one of his legs, and they vanished.

Two men on horseback rode up the road from Bucharest. They spied the body on the roadside and stopped their horses. Warily, they dismounted and crept carefully to the still figure. Hands on swords, they whispered to each other in a language foreign to these lands.

One bent down and looked closely at the lifeless face while the other stood guard, hand on sword hilt.

The first one yelped in surprise, quickly drew his sword, and decapitated the body. He waved the head by its hair, dancing in exultation and triumph. His companion joined in once he'd figured out why.

The two quickly remounted their horses. With the head of their enemy, Count Vlad Dracul, tied to one of the saddles, they tore back the way they had come. In their joy, they never noticed that no blood spurted from their enemy's body when the head was separated from it.

The three returned to stand by the headless corpse. Lucius shook his head.

"Disappointing. But maybe it's better this way. If Vlad's body was still seen wandering around the countryside, there would be a lot more people talking about the undead."

Lilith looked like she wanted to cry.

Lucius peered at Ivan, who had calmed down with the emergence of the dominant being within. Vlad's cruel eyes stared back at him, unafraid. "Still want to die?"

"No."

"We are going to get along well, as long as you remember..."

"...that I serve the Dark One."

Lucius nodded, satisfied. Finally!

A few nights later, after they had fed on a couple of young lovers who had been taking a moonlit stroll, Lucius announced his imminent departure.

"What?" Lilith couldn't believe her ears. "What will we do without your guidance?" She knew full well what she was going to do, but he didn't need to know that.

"I'm sure you'll figure out something. As for me, my part in this little exercise is completed, and the Master wishes me to cause some mischief on the other side of the world. A new continent will be discovered soon, my children, and the seeds of vice, dominance, avarice, and all those other things we hold so dear must be sown in time to wreak havoc on the Creator's handiwork.

"However—a parting command. I charge the two of you to stay together until such time as you have turned a thousand mortals into your own kind. You know how, and you must roam far and wide so that no one is in another's territory."

With that, Lucius disappeared in a vile mix of smoke and brimstone. Lilith and Vlad sat side by side in the moonlight, their victims only a few feet away. They looked at each other in silence.

Vlad leered at Lilith.

Surprised, then pleased, Lilith returned the favor.

Hmm...eternity with this one wasn't going to be so bad after all...

CHAPTER 22

New Orleans
1870

Antoine du Rève stood at a window and stared down at the evening traffic below. The sun was just beginning to set, and its reflection on the water was gloriously brilliant—and deeply irritating.

Carriages drove by, the horses' hooves clopping on the street. People heading home, or to the theater, or out to dinner; all of those mortal distractions that filled their lives and made them happy. All of those things that made him...empty.

Oh, he had tried, ever since he had come to this city He'd resolved to put away his past behavior and make a go at living a "normal" life. So many centuries of stealth, of bloodshed, of death.

Antoine snorted, gazed down at the brandy snifter in his hand. How difficult it had been to put on the characteristics of the living.

Learning to create the illusion of eating, steeling himself against the pain of sunlight, learning to socialize with rather than decimate his neighbors. Letting Cain and Judas be the alphas in turn, and hating himself for it. For a blissful time, though, it had been worth the sacrifice. He had wealth, status, and a companion of sorts.

Now, the age-old hungers were returning. He didn't know why. Maybe it was boredom; hell, it could have been boredom that had driven him to become like mortals. He was fairly certain it was not regret on his, Vlad's, part; neither the turning away from his nature nor the urge to return to it. Regret implied a conscience, and he was sure that he had none. And the other two, Judas and Cain? After all the freedom they had had, they dared not raise an objection. The Dark One would surely send them to torture; he and the Old Man had what would be considered a "close" relationship to those in the world of the living.

Antoine gazed across the street at the dam that kept the river at bay. Boats of all sizes still floated out there, the lights just coming on.

His mind wandered back, as it often did in the evenings. Back to the days when he was still in Romania, high up in the Carpathian Mountains.

Oh, what times he had had! He and Lilith ravaged the countryside, then ravaged each other. There was no end to the villainies one could inflict on a being that could not die. He smiled at the memory.

From the first night away from Lucius, it had been an extraordinary existence. After finding themselves alone, and of course satisfying their lust on each other, the two of them went to Wallachia and thoroughly enjoyed the ruination of every man inside its walls—he for revenge, Lilith simply because it amused her. Those left relatively undamaged either joined them as soulless minions (after, of course, one or two necessary drainings), or were eventually "dismissed"—after a going-away dinner, of course. The pond at the back of the castle became full of bloated corpses, which fed a grateful horde of hungry predators of all types.

As for the townsfolk, they found that their once-secure refuge from the dangers of the forest around them was now more dangerous than the unknown on the other side of the city wall. At first they tried to escape by creeping out under dark of night, to their detriment. However, once the survivors learned that it was the dark that held the terrors, they left during the day in throngs. Many abandoned everything they owned in their haste to escape the horrors that existed in the once-magnificent castle. Of course, they told their terrifying experiences wherever they went, and the strange tales were quick to find the ears of the Hunters.

He and Lilith were blissfully unaware of the dangers that would soon be at their own doors. Night after night, they made good on their bargain with Lucius, and created as many offspring as the countryside could hold. Many of the people in that area, outside of the walls, were perfect for the election. Their auras were an enticing ruby red, with great black holes in the center where their hearts should have been. It was a welcome surprise to find that they were only too willing, once they no longer needed to worry over mortal survival, to spread out to new territories and lay waste to other mortals.

Ever in their bloodied footsteps marched the Hunters. The wood of the Cross found its way into many hideous black hearts, until the last remaining pieces had to be broken down into the tiniest slivers and embedded into the wooden stakes used to deliver the end.

The Hunters also found ways to deter a vampire's attack, often by sheer accident, and many went to affected regions to teach the people how to defend themselves. Once the vampire was weakened by these devices, such as a crucifix, the fiend could be easily backed off and decapitated. Also by horrific accident, they learned never to bury the head with the body; if interred together, both rose in gruesome appearance and, once rejoined, made for an even more horrible, evil monster.

The worst was when the Hunters evangelized their afflicted brethren, so tha in a couple of hundred years the Faith had made it virtually impossible to find easy prey. The spirituality exuded by the populace often made it excruciatingly painful for the undead to enter villages. Eventually, he and Lilith had to evacuate their castle, due to the repopulation of the town by defiant Christians, and take refuge from the Hunters in an abandoned mansion in Austria. They continued terrorizing the populace and replacing their destroyed children, but it seemed as if the Hunters were winning.

So he went north and west, eventually making his way across the English Channel to the British Isles, to settle in the highlands of Northern Scotland, while Lilith chose to flee east to the steppes of Asia. She absolutely refused to leave the lands that she had known from eternity.

Antoine sighed in his musings. How he missed her...

Nevertheless, he had had an interesting career in the Isles. Keeping mostly to the higher elevations and attacking only the lone traveler or obviously lost drunk, he'd stayed inconspicuous for a very long time. Then came the night he decided to visit one of the small villages close to where he made his abode. He had crept up to one door in the dark, and had laid his hand on it to push it open, when pain like a thousand suns suddenly shot through his arm.

He snarled in anger and pain, yanking his hand away.

What in--? He peered more closely, and then jumped back, panicked. He'd almost touched it —a small silver crucifix hanging from a nail on the door. Judas' soul within him cried out in anguish, seeing his betrayal again. Turning, the vampire fled from the place, melting back into the night.

That was when he'd resolved to become like the living; now Antoine remembered. It wasn't boredom or disgust. It was fear. He did it to turn away suspicion and to be able to survive this wave of vampire destruction and defense.

That morning, he stayed alive as long as possible, crouching in the darkest of shade and looking out into the bright sunlight until he could no longer tolerate it. He also caught small animals and forced himself to eat their meat rather than gorge himself on their blood. It took weeks of training his vampiric nature, but he had nothing but time anyway. Finally, he felt he had sufficiently overcome his innate undeadness, and it was time to move on.

First, though, he decided he should probably get some more modern clothes. So, as one last tribute to his true nature, he stalked the familiar roads and killed a couple of wealthy travelers. Looking down at their naked bodies in a shallow grave, he was very proud of himself for having refrained from draining them.

The next day, he emerged from the hills of the Highlands, traveling by day—a well-dressed, comely young man in fine clothes, with plenty of money jingling in his pockets. He was proud of his accomplishments and his looks, although he was disappointed in this body's inability to grow a decent mustache.

He also needed a new name. Since he'd had no companion for over a hundred years, and those victims who he saw fit to turn always left for their own territories, there had been no need for one; and once he realized that the name Vlad was a name that stood out as strange in this country, he felt it best to come up with a new one.

Passing a graveyard on the road to Glasgow, he decided to take a stroll through its grounds in order to find what he needed. As he walked row after row, he observed the names and their commonality.

Thus Vlad Tepes entered the cemetery, and an hour later emerged as Angus Hamilton.

He strode briskly into town, admiring the ancient buildings that had withstood the test of time. "Rather like me," he mused, "only I've weathered better." He laughed softly at his little joke.

Turning in at a tavern on the corner of two busy streets, he sat down in a dark corner and took stock of the patrons. So many dark hearts! So much distress! They would make for a rather interesting dinner, but...

He shook his head. *No, don't think that way.* Blending in and becoming inconspicuous was imperative. Turning mortals into offspring would be just the opposite, eventually.

A busty blonde young lady swiveled herself over to him and bent down to gaze into his eyes. "Anything I can get for you, stranger?" she cooed. The look in her eyes, and the look down her bodice, brooked no doubt that she did not mean that which was on the regular menu. He ogled her, as he knew she expected, then smiled up at her. "Not at the moment, love. Besides, your clientele would miss you."

"My what? Oh, the others." She laughed and waved her hand dismissively. "Doubt it. They've all been in their cups since mid-day." She bent down further and whispered in his ear, "Let me know if you change your mind." Then she gave his ear a nibble and sauntered off.

He watched her go, thinking he might take her up on her offer. The aura around her was a bright red, and had a small black center. With a little work, she might make a good partner and companion. For a while.

The sound of voices raised in argument caught his attention. Two men at the end of the bar, obviously inebriated, were arguing over an object lying in front of them.

"That is as much my invention as yours!" the younger man bellowed.

The older gent, dignified in his high-society clothes and carefully-cropped beard, sat staring at his opponent, eyes flashing. "Listen, MacPherson, you may have helped assemble the thing, but you did not come up with the idea. Be satisfied with your wages, and go. We shall resume the experiments next week."

The other man shrank back, rubbing his arm as if it pained him. Angus, watching them closely, observed something that ordinary mortal eyes would not have noticed. The younger one's arm was pockmarked with a great number of small holes. He got very interested.

"No! No more, Doctor! I refuse!"

"And where shall you find a position that pays as well as I? For if you refuse to help with the tests, you are out of my employment."

"I shall go to London," the younger man retorted. "My wife has a sister there who will keep us until I can find another position." He dashed out of the pub, nearly bowling over two men who were coming in. The doctor watched him go, sighed, and turned back to his drink.

Angus got up and casually walked over to the bar. Sitting beside the downcast old man, he got the bartender's attention. "I'd like a shot of whiskey, and please refill my friend's glass as well."

The bartender nodded, set two glasses of spirits before his patrons, and gladly pocketed the two gold coins that Angus ostentatiously dropped into his hand.

The doctor eyed his new friend through bleary, bloodshot eyes. Angus smiled back, thinking, *Perfect. He's in just the right frame of mind to tell me anything I want to know.*

"Quite an argument you were having there with that young malcontent," he said to his new companion, jerking his thumb back towards the door.

"MacPherson? Oh, yes, the young fool. We have this argument often, and he always comes back." He sighed. "Eventually."

Suddenly the doctor's face blackened with rage, and he slapped his hand hard on the bar, making the man on the other side of him jump in surprise. "That is the last straw," he roared. "I won't have him back. There are important things to accomplish, and now they won't get done. I need to find an assistant I can rely upon."

Angus eyed the object on the bar. "Does it have something to do with this apparatus?"

"Yes." The doctor looked down at the cylindrical item. He picked it up, turning it gently in his hands. "So much still to discover," he murmured, almost to himself.

"What is it, may I ask?"

"This, sir," he held it in front of Angus, "is what is called a hypodermic syringe. It is used to draw fluids out of something, or inject fluids in."

Angus studied the thing. A sharp needle at one end, a hollow cylinder, and a plunger at the other. Quite a simple thing, really...

...and he could already think of several good uses for it...

The old man peered at Angus, a little startled at the wolfish expression on his face. "Pardon my asking, sir, but are you from around here? I've not seen you before."

"Oh, I do beg your pardon. I am remiss in my manners." Angus smiled and extended his hand. "I am Angus Hamilton, new to these parts. My family's lands are just outside Glasgow, and I am here looking for them. Thought I'd stop in here and take care of my thirst." Angus smiled secretly to himself. *Thirst, indeed...*

"And from where do you hail?"

"Ullapool."

"Ah," grunted the doctor. "Explains the accent. My name," he said, taking Angus' hand and shaking it, "is Fergus MacGinley, doctor of medicine, and aspiring inventor."

"Good to meet you." Angus was grateful for the time he'd spent walking in the sunlight; the warmth had brought his skin up to a normal temperature.

They sat in companionable silence for a while. Angus used the opportunity to try to get inside MacGinley's thoughts and convince him to invite him home. It worked.

They walked into the MacGinley home, where Angus charmed Mrs. MacGinley at once.

He was made official assistant by the end of dinner, and the next day started his new job. It was nothing more or less than getting poked by a needle, having various potions and liquid forced into his veins, and letting the doctor record his findings while his human guinea pig writhed and frothed. Of course, none of the experiments had any real effect on Angus, but he thought he ought to do something to make the old man's day worthwhile. When it came to having his own blood taken from him, it rather amused Angus that the tables were turned for the first time since Lilith's fangs had been in his neck.

When he had the chance, he pocketed one of the spare syringes and procured a few needles as well. These he kept in a velvet-lined box under his bed. He began stealing out at night, syringe in his pocket, and relieving his undying bloodlust by extricating the blood of the drunks passed out in doorways. Sometimes he would fill a flask that he carried at all times, other times he would simply squirt the syringe's contents into his eager mouth.

Getting the sustenance he craved became even easier for him when Fergus had to leave town on occasion. It was not difficult to charm Deirdre MacGinley into his bed; she was much younger than her husband, and had a taste for adventure that Fergus did not.

The wine they shared after their nocturnal romps was a special concoction. It was, in fact, along the same lines as the mixture Lilith had given to Angus' second soul, Judas, that long-ago night in Jerusalem. Judas writhed within their shared body, which enraged Angus. However, the sensation passed, as Deirdre lapsed into a happy slumber.

Then Angus would choose an inconspicuous spot on Deirdre's naked, sleeping body and extract as much of her life fluids as he could without killing her. It was fortunate for Deirdre that their liaisons were few and far between, because she was always so listless the next day. It puzzled her greatly, but she would forget it by the time her husband kissed her good-bye and left on another trip.

Angus would have stayed forever, literally, except for rumors he'd heard of Hunters making their way across the Channel. It was only a matter of time. So, giving his apologies to his employer and a bereft Deirdre, he left Glasgow, traveling south and then west to the coast. After selling his horse, which had suffered Angus' extractions on a daily basis, he bought a ticket to the New World.

He managed to control his cravings on the voyage across the Atlantic by helping out in the ship's kitchen. With all that access to the carcasses of slaughtered animals, and no crew member as eager as he was to work with them, he had no end of opportunity to slake his thirst. No one bothered him while he cut up the meat, so he was free with his syringe and flask. However, it was a remote second to what he truly craved.

Occasionally a pretty young thing would give him the eye, and they would end up in her cabin. Any companions, husbands, or chaperones would have been mentally convinced by his powers over their mental faculties to find something else to do during that time. He still had plenty of his potions to put his conquests to sleep, so that he could take what he needed. So, except for a little tiredness on the part of his victims, no one was the wiser.

The first thing he heard when the boat docked in Boston was that the country had declared war on itself. Men in uniform were leaving for the front lines, and he saw an opportunity in following the troops. He knew there would be bloodshed, and he could definitely benefit from the fracas.

Plus, the families of the soldiers followed as well, a swarm of petticoats and lost dreams. He felt it was his duty to comfort the widows, whose population grew every day. He developed a persona that made him look like a weak-hearted cripple; even as a foreigner he knew he would be pressed into service otherwise. This persona kept him out of the battles and safely next to the women and children who would surely need his comfort at the end of the day. He spent his time helping around the camps and tending to the wounded—always with a syringe and flask handy—and at night he would visit the bereaved women.

Most of the time they turned away his attentions at first, but one long look into their eyes and they did anything he wanted. His ability to control their minds surprised him—he knew he'd had the power, but up until now he hadn't known the extent.

Some nights he flitted among the dying on the battlefield, draining them of their blood and taking the money and treasures from their cold bodies before they could be burned or interred in mass graves.

As the war drew to a close, he found himself marching behind new troops to the Gulf of Mexico. At that point, he left the conquering army behind and settled in New Orleans, developing a new persona and changing his name and nationality once again.

At war's end, he was a rich man. He bought a rather large house across the street from the river, and eventually found his way into society as Antoine du Rève. This name was his favorite of all of the people he had been. It translated into the English as "of the dream", but he knew that "revenant" was the French word for "vampire". Yet no one he had ever met even considered the importance, or the danger, behind that name.

He had done the highly important social duty of taking a mistress, one Annelise d'Alondre by name. She was well-known in high society as a lady of wealth, and in lower levels as a lady of the night, and that was why Antoine kept her.

She was almost as depraved as Lilith had been, but of course without Lilith's supernatural powers. Their nights were never without some sort of adventure. He could even extract her blood and drink it in front of her, which excited both of them. He had considered turning her, but rejected that idea for the limitations it would have placed on him. An eternity with the same companion left a bad taste in his mouth; he missed Lilith, but was just as happy on his own.

Even when he bought a coffin and had it set up in a back room, she was unperturbed; in fact, it was the setting for many unholy nights. Once, without realizing it, his fangs had emerged for the first time in decades. Annelise had just laughed, leered at him, and stretched her chin up, pointing to her neck. And, in his bloodlust, he had plunged in, bringing her to the point of death before realizing what he had done. He had pulled away in horror, but she had recovered, smiling weakly as she lay in his coffin. That was the beginning of the end of the experiment in mortality. He had erased Annelise's mind of all that had happened that night, but he couldn't erase his own.

The vampire was back.

CHAPTER 23

"There you are, Antoine, mon chèr."

Annelise flounced over towards him from the doorway, a glass of wine in her hand. From the look on her face, Antoine could tell that she had been availing herself of his supply for most of the evening.

As she got closer, he could hear her heartbeat. It seemed faster than usual, and that both disturbed and excited him. She had been out all day on "errands", and now seemed unable to look straight at him. A smile twitched the side of his mouth as he regarded her with hooded eyes. *What* had *she been up to*, he wondered.

His mistress put an arm around his waist, pushing her body against his. She reached up to nibble his earlobe, and then bit down hard.

She licked at the droplets of blood as he pushed her gently away, and pouted. "What, no fun tonight?" she asked in a little-girl voice.

Then she saw the syringe. Her eyes widened, and her heart hammered in her chest. Antoine was enjoying its rapid rhythm. "Oh, not that tonight, please," she laughed nervously. "I'm all over holes." She moved away from him, visibly tense. "Why, Madame Bertha told me..."

"What??" Antoine interrupted, his face fierce with sudden anger.

Annelise backed away further, stammering with equally sudden fear. "N-nothing, she just saw..."

"WHAT—were—you—doing, seeing that swamp witch?" Antoine demanded, enunciating each word with dangerous clarity.

Annelise gulped, but then her eyes narrowed. "She's not a witch!" she retorted. "She's a voodoo priestess. There's a big difference." The mentally-unbalanced mistress had gone from fearful to indignant in a moment.

"Answer my question!" Antoine stepped toward Annelise, who was trying to negotiate her steps back to the doorway. She knew how Antoine could get when he was in one of these moods, and it was more than even she could bear.

"I'm...it's...female problems. She's good for that sort of thing."

In a cold, measured, and frighteningly quiet tone, he asked, "And what did you tell her about those 'holes'?"

Annelise tried to smile, to reassure him, anything to calm him down. At the same time, she looked furtively around for something near to hand with which to defend herself, if needed.

"Please, Antoine, don't be angry. I told her...I told her I fell into a thorn bush. She believed me, she truly did!" Annelise was speaking in a rush, trying to convince herself as well as Antoine. "She just told me to keep them bathed until they healed. That's all. Really!"

Antoine looked at her, pursed his lips in thought, and then smiled. "Oh, well, all's right with the world then."

Annelise smiled back shakily. She couldn't really tell if he believed her or not, but she was not going to take any chances. His dark moods always ended with her being in pain.

Smoothing her skirts over her hips, she strode briskly toward the door. "Well, then, I'll just leave you to..."

In a blink, Antoine was in the doorway, blocking her escape. A strange, fiery look emanated from his eyes.

"...your...thoughts..." Annelise's voice trailed off as she stared at him in growing fear.

Across the street, a fine cascade of sand and dirt trickled down the side of the earthen dam that kept the impatient water in its place.

"But I am enjoying our conversation. Do let us sit together over here." Antoine indicated the loveseat against the far wall, away from the window.

"I really must—no, I must go, Antoine. I have appointments to keep, and..."

"And you will forget them and stay here." He grabbed her elbow and steered her to the loveseat. She struggled, trying to pull away from his grasp.

"Please let me go!" Her voice was skirting the edge of hysteria. She hit him with her free hand, pulled at his fingers, kicked him, but he paid no attention.

"Certainly, my dear," he laughed, and pushed her onto the cushions.

Annelise cried out when he picked up the syringe. Her eyes wide, she pleaded, "No, please, not that anymore! I...it's just wrong!"

Antoine's eyebrows raised in mild surprise. "Well, well. Are we beginning to have second thoughts about...wait! What is this?" He quickly reached down beside her and picked up a folded piece of paper that was lying on the loveseat. She gasped as she recognized it. Jumping up, she grabbed at it, but Antoine was much faster.

"Give that to me!" she demanded, her voice high with fear. Antoine merely held her back with one arm, holding the other, with the paper, clear out of her reach.

"And what is this, that it is so important that you keep it to yourself? Come now, we shouldn't have secrets from each other." He chuckled, amused at the efforts Annelise was making to retrieve the paper.

"It's just...a note from Miss Bertha, telling me how to treat my...female condition."

Antoine's teasing smile disappeared. "Miss Bertha can't read or write. You told me that yourself." He narrowed his eyes at her, and she shrank in terror from his stare.

"Her...she...I mean, her son can read and write. She had him write it."

"You mean, someone ELSE has seen you?

Annelise fell back onto the sofa, shrinking against it, her arms protecting her from the blows she was certain she was going to receive. "No! No—I mean...she just has these papers written up as general instructions. She has a stack of them..."

"And do they all read, 'How to Recognize and Protect Against Vampires and Other Night Monsters'?" he asked all too calmly.

Annelise gasped and, without thinking, put her arms down to stare at Antoine. He stood over her, the opened flyer in his hand. "So there's a meeting tonight, and you were going to go and learn all about how to keep nightmares from your door. Very bright of you."

He continued in a mocking tone, "Yes, you have so much to fear in this world. With your way of life, Annelise, I should think you would fear more the judgment in the next."

Annelise flushed, anger emboldening her again. "You should talk! The things you do, what you want me to do. What about *your* eternal soul?"

Antoine laughed humorlessly to himself. *Odd you should ask. Which one?*

He faked an attitude of mild contrition. "Well, maybe you're right, dearest. So, no more syringe, eh?"

Annelise nodded, hardly believing the change that had suddenly come over him.

He looked at the device in his hand, shrugged, and tossed it lightly over his shoulder. It fell to the floor, the glass tinkling as it broke into a thousand tiny pieces.

The grains of dirt continued to trickle from one spot in the levee, until it had made a noticeable pile on the street. The amount was still not enough to be alarmed about—this sort of thing happened often—but the passersby moved along a little more quickly when they saw it.

Antoine sat beside his mistress in silence. She watched him, unsure of what he would do next.

He finally spoke, quietly but amiably enough. "So...vampires. Why the sudden interest?" He turned to her and leaned his elbow against the back of the seat, head on hand.

"I just found this—actually, some man accosted me on the street and thrust it into my hands. Oh, Antoine, he looked dreadful. And the scars on his arms!"

Antoine's eyes widened, but he said nothing.

"I was going to throw it away, but..."

"Go on." Antoine's voice was just the same, but there was something in it that caused Annelise to be on her guard again.

"It got me thinking..." It all came out in a rush. "I've never known anyone who keeps a...a coffin...and doesn't have someone, well, in it. And that...when you draw blood, well, it's just not human!"

"Oh, is that it, then?" Antoine exhaled, irritated. "Well, I am tired of this."

"Of what? What did I do?" Too late, Annelise realized she shouldn't have been quite so open.

"You ask a lot of questions. Dangerous questions, if asked to the wrong person."

Annelise broke out into a cold sweat. She jumped up from the cushions and lunged across the room, a scream caught in her fear-frozen throat. He didn't need to say anything, or explain his behavior. With sudden terrible clarity, she knew. She knew!

Once again, her escape was blocked by Antoine, who seemed to fly to the doorway. She screeched, tried to run the other way. He caught her arm and pulled her back, laughing as she struggled to get away. "Oh, Annelise, I can hear your heart hammering frantically, like a small bird caught in a trap. Now would have been a perfect time to have that syringe."

He suddenly grabbed her hair, yanking her around to look at him.

Her face went white as she stared at the fangs protruding from his open, hungry mouth.

Antoine laughed. "I guess I'll have to come up with some other way."

Water began to seep out of the hole made by the dislodging of the dirt. The levee groaned loudly, catching the alarmed attention of the residents up and down the street. Someone tried to shove the mud back where it had come from, but the water pushed it right back out again. Bags of sand, old planks, bits of rags, everything was tried, but the flow of water just kept increasing.

"No! Please! Antoine, don't! I...I won't tell anyone! If you just...leave...I'll tell no one. I'll..."

She suddenly had another idea. "Let me go with you! If you change me into...what...you are, then I'd have to tell no one, and we could be together always! Wouldn't you prefer that? The fun we could have, think about it!!" She was desperate.

Antoine gazed at the vein throbbing in her throat. Annelise's eyes rolled like a lamb's before the slaughter. She tried another tack.

"Those men! The ones handing out the flyers! They must know, or guess, you're here. You...if you...kill me, they will find out! Miss Bertha knows, and she'll send them here!"

Annelise stopped her frantic onrush and gulped. *Miss Bertha! Why did I say that?*

Antoine whispered to her, almost lovingly. "When I leave here tonight, Miss Annelise, I am taking no one besides myself." He was pleased at the trembling and sobbing this information caused her, and added, "Your Miss Bertha will be the first—oh, my mistake—the *second* one to meet her Maker tonight."

Annelise, hysterical by now, squirmed and screamed in terror and desperation. Antoine pushed her up against the wall, tore her throat from chin to collarbone, and had his first fresh human blood in many years.

The seep had become a trickle; the trickle, a small rivulet. Those closest to the site had run back to their homes, wrinkling their noses in disgust as they heard screams coming from the du Rève house. It happened so frequently that they paid it no mind, concentrating instead on saving their belongings.

Antoine threw Annelise's corpse onto the loveseat and strode out of the room. When he got downstairs, he was met with a sharp-toothed attack from Annelise's little poodle. He swept it up off the floor and tore into it, killing it instantly.

Stupid little cur. He'd always hated it.

Now to ready Annelise's final resting place...

He walked to the room in the back of the house where he kept the coffin, occasionally taking sips from the dog as if it was a bottle. Opening the door, he looked in and remembered the debauchery that had been so enjoyable in this room.

He had spared no expense—the coffin was made of imported mahogany, with Chinese silk lining the interior. Too bad he wouldn't be able to use it during the day, but with those men around, whom he was sure were Hunters, he had to relocate yet again.

Absently, he brought the dog to his lips again. Grimacing, he threw the corpse into a corner. There were bigger bodies to ravage tonight.

The water now spurted from the levee, making a small stream that grew larger by the minute. The citizens were near panic, shoving sheets and curtains into the gaping hole.

Suddenly someone shouted, pointing at what was now a small river.

It seemed a miracle, or perhaps a judgment – the water was flowing straight across the street, into the yard of Maison du Rève.

Antoine turned to go retrieve Annelise, but stopped suddenly at the vision before him.

A Being, dressed in a military-style form of clothing, stood in the doorway. "Antoine du Rève," it said. "Or should I say, Vlad Tepes? Angus Hamilton? Cain? Judas? Which one of you is currently in charge?" The being solidified into the image of a young man, golden-haired, regal in his countenance and bearing.

Antoine looked coolly at this stranger. "Who are you, to come into my house without so much as a knock at the door? You, sir, are trespassing..."

"All things are God's, and I have permission from Him to be here," the young newcomer answered.

"What are you raving about? Madman! Get out now!" Antoine roared.

"I will leave when I have performed the duty I came to do."

Antoine crossed his arms over his chest and stared defiantly at this nuisance. "And what, pray tell, might that be?"

The being gazed levelly at Antoine.

"Your time here is finished, Vlad Tepes. Your soul is required."

Antoine's eyes went wide. He backed up warily, readying himself to disappear, as he had often done in the past. Yet he couldn't do it! For some reason, he was powerless before this...

"Who are you, I ask again," Antoine demanded.

"I am Gabriel, who stands at God's left hand, and I have been commanded by my Master to relieve this body of its cruelest burden." Saying this, he produced a small piece of ancient wood.

Antoine gasped, holding his hands over his face, his arms crossed over his chest.

The angel advanced on him, growing larger and more frightening with every step. Antoine had no power to fight him. Gabriel tore Antoine's arms away from their protective embrace, and quickly thrust the stake into Antoine's heart.

The vampire gave a scream of rage and despair, and slumped to the ground. The black soul that was Vlad Tepes writhed from the body and hovered over it. His evil laugh was cut short by a pair of shadows that seeped forth from the ground and pulled him back down with them. He screamed in terror, and then all was silent.

Gabriel turned back to the body, and pulled the wood from its heart. At once the monster awoke again, its visage taking the form of Judas', so long gone from the surface. He pleaded with the angel, "Please, put the stake back! Plunge it in! Let us out too, so we can be free of this existence."

Gabriel looked at the duo with pity.

"You two were too prideful before to acknowledge the Master as Lord of all. You refused to even try to love Him, to see Him as your heart's desire. Has that changed, or does your heart still hold its proud disobedience?"

"We have no master!" both shouted in unison.

Gabriel shook his head. "Not 'Master'—that is the name we angels give Him. Only...'Father'. 'Lord.' 'King.' How hard can it be?"

Judas/Cain snorted. "You were created to obey God without question. How would you know what we've been through? And why we cannot, will not, go to your Master on our knees, nor bow our head to Him."

"Very well. As you wish." The angel turned to go.

The monster stared in disbelief. "So—that's it? We're still free to go?"

Gabriel whirled in the doorway. "I did not say that." He looked at the door, and it slammed shut. Then he faded through the door himself.

Cain/Judas tried to do the same, but Gabriel had caused a seal of some kind. The monster peered through the keyhole, and was surprised to find something blocking it from the other side. He tried to push the object, but screeched in pain when he touched the blockage.

Gabriel's voice came through the door. "It is the wood I impaled you with earlier. You will not be able to touch it." Then a pause, as if he was listening for something. "Ah...it begins."

The house shook as if it were being jostled by a giant. Then Judas/Cain felt the entire structure begin to move—downwards.

The neighbors watched in amazement as a gigantic hole formed around the du Rêve house. Minutes later, there was a rumbling and a wet squelching sound, and the awestruck onlookers watched as the building sank into the hole, mud and water swirling over it. At the same time, the water stopped gushing from the hole in the levee, the stream flowing across the street dried up, and all was normal again.

Except for the gap between the houses where the du Rêve house had stood.

From Book 3:
Resurgence: The Rise of Judas

CHAPTER 1

New Orleans
Present Day

Steve Bronson looked up from his clipboard as his foreman rushed across the street towards him. The New Orleans heat and humidity were taking their toll on the Northwest native; even at its summertime worst, his home state couldn't hold a candle to this torment.

He wouldn't be here at all, except for the strange turn of events that necessitated his organizational abilities. Construction crews rarely faced a situation like this; in fact, he'd never heard of anything quite like what they were having to deal with in this dig. He imagined that protocol everywhere was being rewritten, as details emerged on this lot they were trying to build on.

Preliminary x-rays, now part of the procedure in historically sensitive construction bids, had revealed a large, hollow area five or six feet below where all of the bulldozers and equipment had been sitting just days before. He had been called in because he had had experience with archaeological digs in the past.

"Okay, Sid, what is it?"

The foreman wiped his brow and looked back across the street. "Looks like a roof."

"What??"

"Yeah—like a whole house just sorta sank into the ground."

Steve groaned and turned to his assistant. "Mike, notify the subcontractors. Looks like there'll be a helluva delay. City too. They'll want all interested parties in on it—historical society, whatever. I imagine the archaeologists will get their knickers in a twist if they aren't notified too."

"Got it, Steve. Anything else?"

Steve smiled at the assistant. Such an innocent... "Not for now, but get your phone ready; the shit will be hitting the fan shortly."

Mike looked puzzled, but started making his calls. Steve turned back to his foreman.

"What's it look like?"

"Well, just from a preliminary look, it's in amazingly good shape. Not sure of the age; no one remembers a house ever being there. It was an empty lot before Katrina, so who knows how long it's been there."

"See if there are any areas where we can gain access. Might as well see if there are any other surprises under that roof. I'll have Mike check the city records to find out where the hell this thing came from, and when."

The foreman nodded and trotted back across the road. Steve could hear him barking orders at his men.

Overseeing the almost-surgical proceedings, Steve couldn't help but be impressed by this crew. They seemed to have an almost proprietary attitude toward the dig and the treasure they were unearthing. He looked at the roof pieces, carefully labeled and piled in a safe place, and at the tarp that was put over the exposed roof, a hole neatly cut in it and positioned over the entrance they had made. No doubt about it, this crew deserved much more than they were being paid.

"Who do you have going down?" he asked Sid.

The foreman pointed to two men, already armed with flashlights, oxygen tanks, and gas masks. "Chad and Rene, two of our best. They've been trained in archaeological procedures—even went down to a couple of shipwrecks in the Gulf. I trust them completely."

Steve nodded, and watched as a ladder was lowered into the opening through the roof.

"Be sure to test the flooring. We don't know what stage of rot it might be in," Sid hollered.

The two men nodded, indicating the ropes they had fastened to their waists. The other ends were tied to a nearby backhoe, with two other men standing watch over them. Sid nodded and gave the thumbs-up. Soon Chad and Rene were down the ladder, leaving the rest to wait up top.

Chad turned his flashlight on halfway down the ladder and shined the light around. "Holy cow, would you look at this?"

Rene, two rungs above him, gave a low whistle. "Wow. You'd think folks just up and left a month ago."

Everything they could see was still in place. Not even a window was broken. Dust covered everything, but beyond that it looked like a museum setting.

"Well, keep going. Don't make me stand here contemplating the landscape." Rene tapped his friend's fingers playfully with his foot.

"Okay, okay. Let me test the floor…" Chad climbed down to the bottom of the ladder. He put a foot on the floorboards, tentatively at first, then with his full weight.

"Hunh. Guess no one told the termites about this place." He jumped up and down a couple of times. "Solid."

Rene followed Chad down the ladder to stand beside him. "Still, be careful." His flashlight was now on as well, searching the corners.

"Bet the historical society's gonna want to have this place pulled up in one piece and taken to some other spot. Lady who bought this piece of property is not gonna want to keep it here, that's for sure."

"Helluva fancy basement she'd be getting." Rene snorted. "So much for our crew getting anything done. Might as well go home and break open a few brews." He shook his head and turned to go back up.

Just then, his light cast over a loveseat in the back of the room.

"What the...?" He played the light back over what he'd thought he'd seen. "Oh, hell."

"What?" Chad looked at where the light was pointing. "Lord..."

On the loveseat were the remains of a human body.

"Oh, damnation." Steve squeezed the bridge of his nose, trying to ward off the coming headache. "Where's Chad?"

"Still down there. Saw a hallway he felt needed exploring. I wasn't staying with the skeleton any longer than I had to." Rene was still in the ropes, in case Chad needed help, but the gas mask was off and his face was a ghastly pale color.

Steve peered closely at him. "You okay?"

Rene took a deep breath. "Yeah, I'm all right. Just wasn't expecting it. The stories..."

Steve was instantly on the alert. "What stories?"

Rene looked around, hesitated, then plunged in. He seemed embarrassed at telling the tale.

"Folks 'round here, they won't tell an outsider, but we know. There's a story that says there used to be a grand house here, but it fell into a sinkhole over a hundred years ago. Land has never been quiet since. Folks say you can hear screaming and moaning come up from the ground, and that's why no one's ever built here."

Rene looked as if he needed to put a lot of space between himself and the lot. Steve had questions, however; Rene wasn't going anywhere any time soon.

"You knew about this before the excavation?"

"Yes, sir."

"Yet you told no one."

"I didn't believe the story myself. Then when the roof was found, I thought, okay, well, that don't mean nothing. But when I saw that skeleton..." Rene's hand shook as he wiped his face.

Steve looked at Mike, who nodded. "Already got Forensics on the line. They'll be here within fifteen minutes."

"Okay, good. Now someone get Chad out of there. We need to stay out of the way until the remains have been taken by the forensics people."

Chad's flashlight illuminated the space down the hallway, and he hesitated. He knew he should have left with Rene, procedure being what it was. Overwhelming curiosity got the better of him, though, and he stepped cautiously into the passageway.

The light revealed a door at the end of the hallway, with other doors leading off to the right and left. But it was the one directly ahead of him that caught his attention, because it was the only one that had a huge pile of dirt and bricks in front of it.

"How in the...? he muttered. Flashing his light at the ceiling made him even more puzzled.

No hole in the ceiling, so how did this pile get here? The house had settled evenly, almost deliberately in a way. There was no way for this debris to just magically appear here.

He ventured close to the end of the hallway. Stopping at the edge of the pile, he idly picked up a brick, hefted it, and then put it back. He was about to take out his cellphone and take a picture, when something else odd caught his eye.

The lock mechanism in the door flared for a moment in the flashlight's glare, and Chad took a closer look.

Weird.

There was a piece of wood jammed into the keyhole. It was a fairly decent size, and seemed to have actually deformed the hole.

What kind of force could have caused that? Chad reached over the pile and pulled on the wood. Surprisingly, it came out easily with one tug.

Curious, he shone his flashlight into the keyhole. Would the room beyond be full of treasures, like Tut's tomb, or a big nothing like that gangster-safe thing a number of years ago? Chad completely abandoned the idea of following protocol, clambering up to the top of the debris pile and putting the light and his eye up to the hole.

He jumped back immediately. With a shriek, he fell off the dirt pile and backed away hurriedly. With the wood tight in his grip, he ran with all speed out of the hallway, and didn't stop until he was up the ladder and back to the land of the living.

"A *what??*" Steve was incredulous.

"A coffin! Behind one of the doors!" Chad was panting, as much in fear as in exertion. His eyes were wide and his face pale.

"How odd. Are you sure?" the woman beside Steve asked in a low, almost purring tone.

Chad blinked and stared at her. *Wow! Gorgeous! Raven-black hair, big black eyes, and a figure that didn't know how to stop.*

She glared at his open admiration, but then smiled. "Delilah Atherton. I own this lot."

Her voice held a tone of iron, and something else, which caused Chad to tremble and lose all physical interest in her. *Something wrong here...*He reached into his pocket and grasped the rosary he always carried.

"Um...hi," he managed to stammer. He then turned to Steve.

"There was this door at the end of a hallway, with all this dirt and stuff in front of it," he said in a rush, glancing uncomfortably at Delilah, who was showing far too much interest, "and there was this piece of wood in the lock."

"Wood? What wood?" Delilah's eyes seemed to blaze at this information.

"This." He uncurled his fist, exposing the shard. Steve picked it up, looking curiously at it.

"That's when I looked through the lock, cos I couldn't get the door opened—and that's when I saw the...the coffin..." Chad gulped, looking apologetically at his boss. "I can't go back in there..." he whispered, his voice shaking.

"Not necessary," Steve assured him. "Forensics and the university's archaeological staff will take over from here."

Chad nodded, wiping his forehead, and walked away toward Rene. The two talked animatedly between themselves, glancing at Delilah and looking uncomfortable.

Steve felt Delilah's eyes on him. He looked up from the wood shard and smiled. "Sorry," here he held out the wood to her, "did you want to have a look?"

To his surprise, Delilah jumped back as if burnt. "NO!"

Did she just hiss?? Steve wondered to himself.

She quickly regained her composure. "I...I have a thing about touching dirty things. I can see it fine from here..." She looked at her watch. "Oh, dear, I have an appointment to keep. I'll keep in touch."

And that quickly, she was gone—down the street, into her car, and away.

Steve shook his head in puzzled wonder. *What was that all about?*

A small cough behind him made him whirl around.

Two men stood in the shade, one in a business suit, and the other dressed in khaki shorts and a T-shirt. The suit man spoke.

"Mr. Bronson? I'm Brett Taylor, from the historical society. This is Professor Brian Brown from the university's archaeological department."

"Great! Glad you could both make it so soon. The sooner we get this project tagged, bagged, and out of here, the better for all of us." Steve wiped the sweat from the back of his neck. He missed home, missed Lydia, missed the cooler weather. He knew the evening wouldn't be much better, but at least he could escape into air-conditioned rooms.

His heart dropped at their hesitance to answer. They merely exchanged glances with each other and looked uncomfortable.

The professor spied the article in Steve's hand and gestured at it. "Is that something from the house?"

Steve had forgotten the item. "Oh—right. One of my guys found this in a keyhole."

"In a what?" Brown asked skeptically.

Steve related what Chad had told him, handing the wood to the professor.

Brian looked at it with little interest at first. "Probably just a piece of wall, or—"

Then he peered at it more closely.

"Wait." His voice took on a serious tone as he reached for the glasses in his shirt pocket.

Putting them on, he turned so that the piece was in full sunlight.

"It can't be...," he muttered in growing excitement. He turned to the group of students he had brought with him. They were grouped around the roof samples, notebooks in hand, writing down observations.

"Eugenie!" he yelled.

A young woman separated herself from the group. She looked slightly older than the others; Steve guessed that she was a junior assistant or intern.

"Sir?"

"What can you tell me about this house so far?"

"It looks to have been built about 150 years ago. The ground makes it appear as if it was simply swallowed by a...sinkhole, I'm guessing."

"Anyone been inside, besides the construction crew?"

They heard a curse as two men labored to get a body bag out of the roof hole intact. Brown groaned, "And the forensics team..."

"Yes," Eugenie answered him. We've had a preliminary sortie down there. Seems everything is intact, down to the books and knick knacks on the shelves. Weird."

"Any wood that looks like this?" He held out the shard.

Eugenie touched it, hesitated, then took it from Brian.

"This came from down there?" she asked, eyes wide.

"Yes. Why?" Steve was catching some of her excitement.

"This shard's *ancient*. Well, at least much older than the house. I'll have someone go down and see if there is anything that looks like this, just to be sure."

Brian said, "I'll take the wood back to the lab and run some tests."

Steve nodded and reached for his wallet. "Here's my card. Let me know what you find out as soon as you can."

"Will do." The professor turned away, going back to his knot of students. Eugenie was having a hard time convincing the group to volunteer for the fact-finding mission. They had all seen the body bag, and had heard about the coffin.

Steve turned to speak to the historical society representative. "And what can I do for you?"

"We'd like to have copies of any and all information, pictures, test findings—all pertinent information. It is our hope to exhume the house and put it on the state's list of historical sites, but we have to have the proof before we can get state or federal grants to even start an excavation."

Steve sighed and handed out another card, which Taylor took. He put it into his pocket. "Thank you. We'll be in touch." He turned on his heel and went back to his car.

"Mr. Bronson?"

Now what...

The coroner had walked up behind him. Steve turned, eyebrows raised.

"We have removed the body. And we did find the coffin. I have a team coming tomorrow to examine it and the rest of the house. Until that is done, I'm afraid all activity must cease at this site."

Steve rolled his eyes. Another night snuggled up to a bottle of headache pills... "Did you find anything inside, the, uh..."

The coroner looked uncomfortable. "No, none of my staff would open it. Superstitious bunch."

"Ah. Understandable," Steve agreed. He signaled to Mike. The assistant nodded in turn, and spoke to the crew lounging around in the shade. They moved off to their cars, some looking back sadly, others pairing off to head to the nearest bar.

Steve watched them go. He felt bad for them; they were a really good bunch and needed the work. When he got back to corporate, he'd see what he could do about getting them paid some sort of compensation for the time they were delayed here.

The lot was deserted, the roof pieces carefully laid back over the hole. Temporary chain-link fence had been brought in and hastily erected around the entire site.

As evening approached, the only living being left there was a security guard. He sat in his car with the doors locked, slumped down in the seat so as to be less noticeable. This was a really bad neighborhood to be found in at night without some sort of protection. A firearm, which was all the guard had on him, was not nearly enough to keep the denizens of these blasted and rickety buildings at bay. He sat, unmoving, praying to survive until midnight, when the next unlucky stiff got to take over.

Inside the underground house, a low rumbling started. The foundations did not shudder; the chandeliers were still as death. Through the floorboards rose dark wraiths. Some solidified into formless black masses, taking on substance. Others, lighter, less ponderous, formed into what looked like round, floating sea urchins. Blacker than the memories of the worst nightmares, they skittered on the ceiling and walls. Occasionally they would emit quick flashes of lightning.

Once the mists stopped rising through the floor, the emissaries of Hell moved purposely through the rooms, seeking.

They gathered in the hallway that led to the door with the coffin behind it. Swarming over, around, and through each other, the entire mass thundered toward the door, the shadows moving thickly across the floor, the black orbs fluttering across the walls. They reached the end of the hall, and the dirt and bricks exploded into dust. The door flew open for the first time since the late 19th century, and the blackness overran the coffin within.

Suddenly the lid of the coffin shattered. Pieces of wood flew up and out, raining down to the floor in a torrent of clatter. Part of the group of shadows separated itself from the rest and dissolved back into vapor. It drifted over the inert body in the coffin, and with sudden precision forced its way into the mouth and nostrils of the apparently dead form.

A groan, and the body sat up. The eyes opened, looked around at its surroundings, then saw the open door.

With a scream that came from years of frustration, anger, madness, and, above all, unrelenting hunger, the creature flew out of the room.

The monster had arisen.